TRAVIS & THE LABYRINTH

Matt Shore

THE ORPHANAGE

Nestled in the southern forest of Krankfert in an isolated village called Mercy Square there was a skinny boy with sandy-blonde hair named Travis. Travis was an orphan. He lived in Mercy Square's ramshackle orphanage, along with two-dozen other children whose parents were dead, missing, or simply did not want them. It was a quiet life of daydreams and doldrums, aside from the rantings and ravings of the orphan keeper, Vonkenschtook.

Vonkenschtook was an oblong man with a ruddy throat. Due to poor dental hygiene Vonkenschtook's phlegm was so severe that he often sounded like he was yodeling. This made listening to him severely unpleasant, beyond the fact that he never had anything pleasant to say.

"Listen here, you little snot-weasels," Vonkenschtook had said one morning. His declarations usually meant new rules, which in turn meant new reasons to punish the orphans. Standing in the center of the orphans' shared bedroom, he had told them all, "You are hereby forbidden to speak to the people in town. I don't want you lot spreading any more lies about me. I have been fatherly and kind to each of you, even those of you who barely deserve it."

This was when Vonkenschtook shot a suspicious look at Travis. The other orphans followed his gaze and mimicked the man's scorn, muttering to one another about what a rotten stink-beetle Travis was. Travis merely sighed and shook his head, letting his locks wobble to-and-fro. After years of Vonkenschtook's contempt, Travis was used to this sort of thing. Rather than meeting Vonkenschtook's eyes, Travis tried to find a friendly crack in the floor, hoping that acting innocent might help him avoid another unwarranted walloping on the noggin.

Vonkenschtook grumbled in Travis's direction, but it seemed as though Travis was merely a diversion. After shuffling his tongue around a bit, Vonkenschtook continued his rant.

“I have heard from Gunther, that arrogant woodsman who's always strutting around the village as if he were the Queen. He said that two of you scum-flies told lies about me in exchange for biscuits. As if my cooking wasn't enough to sate you! I provide the very best! But you told him that I serve you slop? Outrageous! Let's just see what you get!"

The orphans went wide-eyed and gritted their teeth in anticipation of whatever the tyrant had planned. With a turn of his heel, Vonkenschtook approached the only upright piece of furniture in the room, a bed that the children had cobbled together from split logs, broken planks and straw. Vonkenschtook raised his mud-painted boot above the bed while the children gaped in horror. Down came his foot, again and again, crash, crash, *CRASH!* Vonkenschtook stomped the bed to pieces.

Though Travis was unpopular amongst the other orphans and had never been allowed to sleep in the bed, he was horrified on everyone’s behalf. He'd known Vonkenschtook to be cruel, but this seemed extreme even by the orphan keeper’s standards. Travis felt a strange sensation. It was like Balien Road, the Fate of passion, was burning within his heart, surging with fiery fury at the sight of this injustice. As he watched Vonkenschtook stomp the bed flat, Travis's fists trembled with anger. *I wish I could punish you, Vonkenschtook,* Travis thought. *One day, when I am grown, I will come back here and teach you a lesson.*

But a pang of anxiety within Travis's mind made him wonder if he would ever have the opportunity to leave the orphanage at all, let alone return.

As the bed crumbled to bits, Vonkenschtook wheezed and clutched at his chest, short of breath. The orphans wept and clung to one another, trying hard not to make too loud a whimper for fear of catching the man's attention. The orphan keeper grumbled, rubbed his head, and exited the orphans' bedroom, slamming the door, as if the moment had passed and no more needed to be said.

Though they were relieved to see him leave, the orphans knew well enough that this reprieve might be temporary. Certainly there were times when Vonkenschtook seemed studious, hard-working, and reliable, but there were other times when his rage unbridled him from reality. Once his tantrums began, there would be no quelling them until he disappeared into his study, where he would usually write a furious letter of grievances to the world at large. He would then read the letter to the orphans with booming oration, over and over, until they begged him to stop. One time he had shouted so loudly that the paintings had fallen off the walls. At least, that was what Travis's friend Rooty had told him.

Travis dreamed of escaping this wretched place, leaving the hard stone walls of Mercy Square behind and exploring the forest beyond. His deepest desire was to visit the Clockwork City, the capital of Krankfert, where the Princess lived. The other orphans often spoke of how beautiful the city was, and how rotten it was that they'd never get to see it. It was their lot in life to live and die in Mercy Square.

Travis tried to memorize every fact about the Clockwork City that he could discover, however poorly vetted or unverifiable it may have been. Most of his worldly knowledge came from the only book he owned. It was an old tome he'd "borrowed" from Vonkenschtook's study called *Wonky's Krankferten Monsters*.

Travis had snuck into the study while Vonkenschtook was berating another orphan for sneezing too loudly. The study was a small, cramped room packed to the brim with books. The books seemed to give Vonkenschtook wild ideas, but they also resulted in a lot of excess chores for the orphans. Once Vonkenschtook had read a book on military strategy during the Grimalkin wars, then came bursting forth from his study declaring that the orphans would henceforth be required to perform rigorous combat drills every morning. This was why many of the orphans hated books and refused to learn how to read. They blamed books for Vonkenschtook's outbursts. Some of them even wanted to burn his study down, though they could not work out how to do so without setting the whole orphanage ablaze. Travis knew how to read and loved to do so, but that fact made him even more ostracized. He assumed that his mother or father had taught him how, but he could not recall enough of his past to be certain.

Before he'd read *Wonky's Krankferten Monsters*, Travis's eyes had been relatively closed. He had only known of the town he lived in, Mercy Square, the forest of No Mercy that surrounded its walls, and the jarters, a ravenous red ape horde that stabbed humans with their barbed tails. They were taken for granted in this region, and were the reason few villagers ventured beyond the city walls. As a result of the jarters, few visitors ever arrived in Mercy Square, and those that did had little positive to say about the place that might inspire future tourism. Once Travis had started reading the book, his mind began buzzing with possibilities.

Travis wanted to see the spire of the Princess's Tower in the Clockwork City. He imagined the Princess in his mind every day as he gazed out the window at the trees, hoping somehow to catch a glimpse of her, though he knew deep down the distance made it impossible. Still, he could picture her so clearly in his mind. She would have a blue crown with many horns. She would wield a gilded scepter used to strike her foes in the head. Her hair would be larger than a horse, and it would dance through the air like ribbons in the breeze. He was certain his vision of the Princess was accurate, though it was based solely on rumor and speculation.

On the morning that Travis turned thirteen years of age, he decided that he'd had enough of dreaming, wishing, and wanting. From that day forward he would dedicate himself to escaping the orphanage at all costs.

"Today," he proclaimed to the others, "I am a man of thirteen. You must all respect me as a man from now on."

This of course was grounds for a savage beating from the other orphans. Who was Travis to declare himself "a man?" He was a sniveling worm like the rest of them, and after a few socks to the jaw, kicks to the ribs, scratches to the cheek and arms, Travis realized that saying some words and accomplishing a deed were two completely different things.

They do not understand me, Travis thought, curled up in a ball of bruises. *I shall keep my plans to myself.*

The other boys hadn't really meant to hurt him, just to teach him his place and to remind him that he was no better than they were. But the lesson had failed to stick. Travis, though slightly bloodied, was inspired by this beating to work even harder to escape. Why should he hang around a bunch of louts willing to club him for declaring his heart's purest wish? Sure, they were all starving for familial love and desperate to hide any sign of weakness, but that did not mean Travis had to consign himself to their short-sighted worldview. He knew, he just KNEW, that something different was waiting for him outside the walls of Mercy Square, and even if it wasn't perfect, it had to be better than Vonkenschtook.

Rooty, Travis's lone friend, tried to soothe his bruised body, rubbing his sore spots gently with a living snake that she'd caught in the bushes outside.

"Are you sure this is working?" asked Travis, wincing.

"Hush," said Rooty. "You need to soak up its slime or you'll never get better."

Travis was not convinced that Rooty was particularly skilled in animal care or medicine, but seeing as she was the only one willing to speak to him without pummeling him, he decided to accept her remedy. After all, when a person only has one friend, the quality of that friend matters less than the fear of losing them.

Rooty and Travis had become fast friends when Travis first arrived at the orphanage, mainly because Rooty felt sorry for him. Vonkenschtook seemed to hate Travis with a particular vengeance, as though he were an imposition. But despite the orphan keeper's penchant for ranting, he was oddly mum about Travis's origins, as if the mere thought of the tale shook Vonkenschtook to his core. So instead he filtered his emotions through a funnel of contempt, and that slow drip of cruelty inspired the other orphans similarly.

Rooty knew about exclusion and derision firsthand. She was the only girl in the orphanage and had worked to avoid being excluded from activities. She had decided to outdo the boys at everything they did by being rougher and filthier than they were. She would have had dark brown hair naturally, but it had purpled due to moss from all the time she spent sleeping in bushes. She often found spiders in her hair, much to her delight and Vonkenschtook's revulsion. He used to hit her with the only spoon in the orphanage to drive the spiders out, but one time they ended up crawling across the spoon toward his fingers, and he shrieked and relented. After that, Vonkenschtook just sort of avoided Rooty, as if she were unfixable.

Beyond being outcasts, Rooty and Travis shared a fascination with insects and arachnids and all the other little crawly-things of the forest. In fact, Rooty had amassed a small horde of rickticks, click-back beetles that could be taught to race. As a result of this, she'd recently gained popularity for her inventing an event she called Ricktick Rumble. At his most lonesome, Travis worried that he might lose his only friend now that Rooty had developed an attractive quality. Travis hoped that he could improve his own popularity by competing and winning in Ricktick Rumble, but based on his sour luck, Travis was having a great deal of difficulty remaining confident.

On Travis's thirteenth birthday Vonkenschtook clumsily created a meal to feed all twenty-five of the orphans. Based on the hasty nature with which Vonkenschtook prepared it and the lack of discernibly edible ingredients, Travis assumed that there would be no birthday treat. In fact Travis believed that the main ingredient in all of Vonkenschtook's cooking was either dirt or sand.

"Sit down immediately," Vonkenschtook shouted to the orphans.

Not even the birthday boy was free from Vonkenschtook's militaristic regimen. While Travis considered the reason for

Vonkenschtook's ill-will, Vonkenschtook bopped him on the noggin with the orphanage's only spoon. Travis grimaced and seated himself on the ground where he belonged.

All of the orphans were soon seated or crouched around the dilapidated table, more a cluster of planks and nails than a sturdy piece of furniture. Vonkenschtook had invented a recipe for an extremely low-cost dish he called "gwish" which looked like grey vomit. The children hated its silty taste, but if they tried to sneak away from the table, Vonkenschtook would punish them by locking them in the basement with no light until he remembered that they were down there. It was so terrible and terrifying in the basement that the orphans no longer risked it, instead gobbling up their gwish- whatever it was- while forcing a smile for the chef. Most of the boys ate it cold off the table.

When Vonkenschtook began plopping glops of gwish before the orphans, his decrepit assistant Needle meandered over to the table holding the orphanage's sole plate. From the eerie, senile look in Needle's eyes, Travis could tell that the old man had an idea, and that whether he intended it or not, this idea would likely result in trouble. With a shaky but somewhat grand flourish, Needle placed the treasured plate before Travis, and bowed creakily.

"Tis the boy's birthday," said Needle, matter-of-factly.

Needle began humming happily to himself, squinting so severely his eyeballs were barely visible. The other orphans stopped forcing gwish down their gullets and gaped at this anomaly. Vonkenschtook's eyes bulged.

"You mindless git," cried Vonkenschtook, snatching the plate away. "A birthday is no excuse for kindness. Especially not to that creature."

Travis hadn't even had a chance to touch the plate before Vonkenschtook had taken it back. Vonkenschtook polished the plate with a vengeance, using the misbegotten rag hanging from the rope around his gut.

“Who knows what vile vectory is piping within this malcontent," Vonkenschtook mused as he stroked the plate lovingly, trying to rid it of whatever foul curse Travis might have placed upon it. “I cannot take such risks.”

And with that, Vonkenschtook snapped the plate in half, ensuring that no one would ever get the honor of using it again.

The other children gasped. Needle sputtered some spittle out through his thin yellow teeth onto the white spiky strands of his beard.

"You forced me to do it, Needle," said Vonkenschtook. “You know I have no patience for chicanery. Especially regarding *that one*.”

Vonkenschtook's eyes turned to Travis briefly then darted away.

That was when Travis had a startling realization. *He fears me*, Travis thought, shocked by how the fear was reflected in the fumbling of Vonkenschtook's hands, his inability to make eye contact, and his repeated refusal to speak Travis's name.

In spite of the snapped plate, Travis could not help but smirk. How could this pompous old orphan keeper be afraid of him? Even if Travis had called himself a man, he was still a much smaller man than Vonkenschtook. To an orphan, Vonkenschtook was a towering pot-bellied ogre. *He could smash me to bits like that broken bed upstairs*, Travis thought.

But there it was, clear as day, *fear* in old Vonkenschtook's eyes. Suddenly a memory flashed in Travis's mind. He had seen that look before, in his father's eyes, on the day his parents had died. Travis had only been four years old, so the memories were spotty at best, but he remembered the heat of the flames that had consumed his family, and he remembered his father's eyes.

What happened that night? Travis wondered. *Was it just a normal fire, or some feat of vectory? Is that why Vonkenschtook is so afraid?*

In the common parlance of Krankfert, a 'Vec' was someone who manipulated the particles around them to perform supernatural spells, or 'vectory,' as it was known. Vector was said to be the force of magic that operated in various forms in all manner of existence. Vecs, or vector users- wizards, witches, and mages, as they were known to the rest of the world- were those who could manipulate the shape and function of the natural world through the power of an elemental aura within them. In doing so, they could seemingly manifest the impossible. As a result, Vecs were hated and feared in the kingdom of Krankfert by the common people. Vectory had been outlawed for years.

This made little sense to those science-minded adventurers who dreamt of unlocking the secrets of the world's core, which they believed to be a sphere of pure vectory more powerful than any other. Travis liked to imagine such things to keep his spirits up, especially in times like these, when Vonkenschtook's rage made him particularly unbearable.

With a single sweeping motion, Vonkenschtook knocked the gwish off the table and onto the floor, where the more obedient orphans began gobbling it up all the same like hungry hogs.

"That's enough gorging for you lot," said Vonkenschtook. "You can thank- eh, *that one*, for the meal's abbreviation. Outside with you! But not too far, or I shall have your heads on a pike by sundown!"

The orphans raced outside, excited by this moment of unsupervised recess. Rooty grabbed Travis by the shoulder, pulling him alongside her, out through the sitting room and into the cloudy, breezy daylight.

From beneath her tunic Rooty revealed that she'd smuggled Travis's book outside so the two of them could enjoy it together.

"Sorry to pilfer this from you," said Rooty, "but I figured you might want a bit of a birthday pick-me-up. Let's try to find the weirdest thing in here, eh?"

Rooty was the one person in the orphanage with whom Travis shared his *Book of Creatures.* Together the duo had spent many an hour pouring over the book's vivid imagery and its descriptions of magical beings. Just the other day, they had gotten into a disagreement about the existence of creatures called viledarts.

"One time a kid got adopted by viledarts," Rooty said. "They walked up in human costumes. Vonkenschtook was so greedy he sold them two kids, no questions asked. Later that night, the viledarts drank their blood like this."

Rooty made a hideous slurping noise, and proceeded to flap her arms like wings.

According to *Wonky's Krankferten Monsters*, viledarts were terrifying bat-like creatures that lived in the swamp and lurked on two legs. They apparently liked to dine on human flesh. They were one of many reasons why Travis and the other children were too frightened to venture into the dark forest of No Mercy.

A CHIVALRIC TALE

The forest was known as No Mercy because of its extreme danger. Mercy Square was an oasis of sorts, relatively speaking, located deep within its center, far from the main road that led northwest to Clockwork City and southeast to Southerner's Roost. The only time the children were allowed to leave the city walls was when they were led by Vonkenschtook on his tedious exercise drills.

Each time before they left, Vonkenschtook would remind the children about the jarters. The jarters were fierce red oblings. They had sharp red horns on the tops of their heads. Some had spiked tails. The tails could whip and sting a person to death. Vonkenschtook said that a swarm of jarters could kill a man in seventeen seconds. After an incident a few months prior, Travis doubted Vonkenschtook had any experience with the creatures at all. Travis had seen a jarter tail sticking up from the brambles in the forest, and he'd called out to Rooty to come see it too, but by the time Vonkenschtook arrived with the others the tail had disappeared. Vonkenschtook had climbed atop a stump to survey the spot, and upon seeing no jarter had bopped Travis thrice with the spoon.

After a half-hour of paging through *Wonky's Krankferten Monsters* in the alleyway behind the orphanage, Travis and Rooty heard Needle call the children back inside. Their reprieve from scheduled torture had been short-lived. Wednesdays were story days, and the person telling the stories was Vonkenschtook, meaning the stories were miserable.

Vonkenschtook's tales always had the same hero, a pompous knight named Vonkenbrandt who rode a pure white stallion called Harriet. On the afternoon of Travis's thirteenth birthday, Vonkenschtook sat the orphans down and told them the story of how Harriet died.

"Vonkenbrandt was walking through the woods," Vonkenschtook said. "Harriet had left him in the night, being a stupid and thoughtless creature."

The orphans were gathered around Vonkenschtook on a straw-covered portion of the wooden floor. Vonkenschtook sat atop a small stool in the center.

"'Harriet,' the knight Vonkenbrandt cried, 'Harriet, where are you, my loyal steed?' but Harriet the horse was nowhere to be found."

The orphans were astonished. Normally Harriet was Vonkenbrandt's loyal companion. They were inseparable, sort of like Travis and Rooty.

"You see," Vonkenschtook explained, "Vonkenbrandt had overslept from eating too many gupperfruit."

Travis tried not to laugh, but he emitted a small snort. Gupperfruit, or gups, as they were commonly known, were a tomato-like fruit that hung from trees. It was frowned upon for children to taste the gups, because they were known for a mead-like intoxicating effect, which resulted in a person becoming wobbly, overconfident, and generally likely to say or do stupid things.

"What's so funny, you little ape?" Vonkenschtook spat at Travis.

"I'm sorry," Travis said, trying to smooth things over. "I just- you always say that Vonkenbrandt is a noble knight."

"He was," Vonkenschtook said. "The noblest, most vigorous fighter in the land."

"Then why did he stay up late getting drunk on gups?" asked Travis.

The other orphans laughed. It was unlike Travis to be so directly confrontational with the orphan keeper. Was he really so dedicated to acting like "a man" that he would set himself up for punishment?

Vonkenschtook stammered, as if he'd been caught in a contradiction. "Ah- hm- silence! No talking during the story or I'll make a new story about how I buried you out back," he decreed.

Travis was unsatisfied with this answer. He wondered if Vonkenschtook was making this story up as he went along.

"Vonkenbrandt wouldn't normally have been eating gups," said Vonkenbrandt, his eyebrows twitching while he spoke. "But he was- yes, he was so torn up inside because Harriet was missing that he took to the fruit to comfort him in his time of sorrow."

Vonkenschtook sat back a little, self-satisfied. A few of the orphans exchanged looks of confusion and murmured to one another.

Rooty waved her hand in the air for attention. "But you said Harriet left while he was asleep. How could he be sad that she was gone before she went missing?"

Some of the other orphans nodded and agreed. Vonkenschtook looked sweaty and uncertain now, as if he'd been cornered by an unruly mob.

"S- silence," Vonkenschtook demanded. "Or I'll get the spoon and bop the lot of you. Do you hear me? This is my story. Mine!"

The kids quieted down. Vonkenschtook's green eyes stared unblinkingly at the children. He glanced at Needle for support, but Needle was already asleep on the floor, curled up like an old hound.

"Vonkenschtook had shirked his duty in caring for Harriet," Vonkenschtook said.

"You mean Vonkenbrandt?" asked Rooty.

"That's what I said," Vonkenschtook stumbled. "Vonkenschtook- Vonkenbrandt, I mean. He- instead of taking care of his horse like he should have, he was selfish and became drunk. And so Harriet the horse was lost in The Burnt Wood."

The children emitted little noises of panic.

"This is terrible," Travis said.

"Yes," Vonkenschtook agreed, hoping to be back on track. "A terrible fate befalls anyone who shirks their duty. A lesson you had best remember."

"No," Travis said, smirking. "I meant your storytelling is terrible."

The other children burst out laughing. Even Needle chuckled in his sleep. Vonkenschtook looked as though his hair might catch fire from rage.

"Silence!" Vonkenschtook roared. "All of you be still!"

And so Vonkenschtook was forced to get the spoon and bop each one of them, then Travis several more times, until they agreed to listen quietly. Once they were settled, Vonkenschtook diverted from his story for a brief tirade.

"Just because it is one's birthday does not mean that one may speak his mind! I am your superior, you lowly, uncouth wretches! You would do well to learn that you were born from nothing and can be cut down just as easily."

Travis stayed silent, but his mind was on the precipice of a realization.

"Now where was I? Ah yes. Here's what happened..."

Travis was struck by an epiphany. Vonkenschtook's stories were fiction. Bad things happened to Vonkenbrandt the knight, because Vonkenschtook perceived the world to be a terrible place where bad things happened at random. Vonkenbrandt never took responsibility for himself, only blaming the ills of the world on others. Of course Vonkenschtook had created him.

"Vonkenbrandt searched for many hours, but he could not find Harriet," said Vonkenschtook. "Then, when his legs were sore and aching, he came upon a clearing where he saw Harriet laying perfectly still. He placed his hand upon Harriet's ribs, but they were cold. The horse was not breathing. She had died."

Some of the children began crying, but Travis no longer believed these lies. If Vonkenschtook had made it all up, Travis could easily make up his own story in which Harriet was alive and well. Wanting to save the others from their emotional suffering, he spoke up again.

"It's not true," Travis said, standing up and addressing the others.

"Quiet," said Rooty. "I've been bopped on the noggin enough for one day."

"But don't you see? He made it all up," Travis explained. "His name is Vonkenschtook and the knight's name is Vonkenbrandt. It's all make-believe!"

"What?" Rooty shouted. "Piltik's poison feet! I thought it was real!"

The children began to boo and hiss at Vonkenschtook for lying, which woke Needle from his slumber. After listening to their complaints and eying the uncharacteristically silent Vonkenschtook for answers, Needle suggested:

"Perhaps some elements of the tales are fictional, but they are meant to inspire you, and remind you that the spirit of a knight lives in every child."

For whatever reason, this was the last straw for Vonkenschtook.

"Absolute rubbish," Vonkenschtook cried. "None of these children are as noble as I am! I mean, as noble as Vonkenbrandt and I both are. You're being misled by this little traitor! I've had enough of your betrayal! To your sleep-sacks, all of you, before I build a new stool from your bones!"

Vonkenschtook forced the orphans back upstairs to their dormitory and locked them inside, where the people of town would try to ignore their screams.

THE DEATH OF GOLIATH

After Travis had freed them all from story time, Rooty convinced the orphans that this was an opportunity for Ricktick Rumble. The orphans happily agreed, as racing insects was as close to adventure as any of them had ever gotten. Using fragments of wood and broken materials she'd gathered, old pots and metal hinges, busted wheels and buckets, Rooty had fashioned an intricate but deadly racetrack for insects, which she called Ricktick Rumble.

There were rickticks crawling all over the flora beyond the walls, thick black beetles about the size of an adult human's thumb. They had little wobbly antennae that they used to sniff out food. Following a ricktick was an excellent way to find treats. Once the orphans saw a ricktick scuttling about they would follow it to its food source then snatch the ricktick up for use in the racetrack. Flower buds and petals were also an enticing treat for insects, less so for children, so the orphans would collect them to place at the end of the track. It was the perfect way to incentivize an insect to race.

Ricktick Rumble was a top-of-the-line, one-of-a-kind bug course so complicated that only a miniature madwoman like Rooty could have concocted it. Bugs would crawl up a broom handle to the high shelving on the wall, where there would be a second ramp, by way of a short wooden plank, leading up through the busted out mouth hole of an unflattering drawing of Vonkenschtook. Rooty had taken extra care to paint a likeness of the man using mud and berry juice that truly captured his nature, right down to the goiter on his neck.

After the drawing, the bugs would crawl around a series of broken flower pots, weaving between them. They were cracked in a triangular fashion, hand-picked by Rooty from other people's refuse to resemble mountains. She referred to this area as Storm Mountain Pass because she was a bit theatrical.

After Storm Mountain Pass, the bugs would tightrope walk over The Sunken Temple, represented by a rope tied across a bucket of water. If the bugs made it across the cord they would reach a twisted tree branch infested with snapworms, tubular pink insects covered with spines. They were known for sticking three-quarters of their bodies from a hole or crack and then slapping their spines into potential prey. They could snap quickly and stick to a ricktick's back, piercing its carapace and dragging it back into a hole to feed upon it. They were only a mild danger to humans, but to a ricktick they were deadly. The branch was the final challenge of Ricktick Rumble before the finish line, which was represented by a small piece of fabric on the ground with the word FIN painted on it in blood. Rooty had wanted to spell the word 'FINISH' in full, but had mismanaged her space and had not felt like bleeding enough to try again.

Other than that blunder, Rooty took the whole thing very seriously. Before she'd gotten started she'd used the same twisted branch, back when it had been a bit fuller, to pry open a cracked wooden wall panel in the children's bedroom and create for herself a secret storage chamber. She kept all the track materials inside so that Vonkenschtook couldn't find them. She even had a secret signal, two fingers to her eyes, then two fingers in the air, to let the other orphans know to quickly and quietly break down the race track and stow it in the wall. She was something of a spymaster for so young a child.

Travis had enlisted Rooty as his mentor to help him find the best bug in Mercy Square. After weeks of searching they'd eventually settled on a thick black beetle called Goliath. Travis treated Goliath like a treasured family pet. To Travis, Goliath was his ticket to popularity.

As the children prepared the racetrack, Travis retrieved Goliath from where he'd concealed him in his sleep-sack and carried the ricktick in clasped hands towards the starting line. Rooty was barking orders at the younger orphans.

"You remember what the track looks like, don't you?" She asked them. "Or do I have to set it up myself every time?"

Two of the younger dunderheads, Miff and Fortune, pretended to listen to her but were too busy screwing around to take anything seriously. Miff turned to grab something from the secret storage space and ran directly into Fortune, who was walking in the opposite direction. They both fell to the ground hugging one another for support. As soon as they hit the ground they began wrestling, taking out their embarrassment on each other. The other orphans stopped working on the track and watched the debacle. They cheered for the fighting children as Rooty shouted for them to stop. But it was no use. Once locked in combat, the two boys could not be pried apart, and the cheering of the crowd only egged them on further.

Travis decided to take Goliath back to his corner so he could coach the bug with a pre-race pep talk, but as he turned away from the wrestling match, Travis likewise ran head first into someone else. Only this someone was so tall that Travis's head only came up to this person's chest. It was Gulken, the youngest of the three elder orphans, around sixteen years of age. Gulken had red-brown shaggy hair that cascaded down in waves, and when he scowled down at Travis, it seemed as though Travis was staring at a monster. Gulken had taken Vonkenschtook's lessons about Travis to heart, meaning Gulken treated Travis like scum.

"Sorry, uh, Gulken," Travis said. "I was just-"

"What's that?" Gulken asked, pointing at Travis's hands.
"It's- it's a secret," Travis said.

Travis immediately regretted his choice of words. This would no doubt pique Gulken's curiosity and result in something unfortunate.

"It's my birthday. I'm so special," said Gulken, prancing around in mockery.

Pouncing like a lion, Gulken clasped his large hands around Travis's tiny ones and squeezed with considerable might. Travis could feel Goliath squishing and cracking under the pressure of Gulken's thumbs.

"Stop," Travis said. "You'll kill him!"

But Travis felt the crack, *CRACK* and the gooey residue as Goliath died in his hands. Gulken had squeezed the poor bug to death. Travis's birthday wish, his hope of winning a race, had died.

Travis pulled his hands apart, and all that was left was some sticky goo and bug bits. He howled with horror, then wiped his hands on his clothes, but that only smeared the mess around and made him feel sick inside. *He's a murderer*, Travis thought. *Someone should squish Gulken! Oh, if only I were bigger.*

"That's what you get for thinking you're special," Gulken said.

Travis had wanted to slap that dumb smile off of Gulken's face. But had he wanted to, Gulken could've squished Travis just like Goliath. Knowing Vonkenschtook, Gulken probably would have gotten away with the murder too. And so Travis ran back to Rooty, trying not to cry for his fallen pet's fate.

"Gulken- he killed Goliath," Travis said. "Or made me kill him. Or-"

"Yeech," said Rooty, inspecting the gooey mess. "Disgusting."

Travis tried to puff out his chest and remain manly while sniffling, but a tear dripped down his cheek and landed on his bare foot.

"Don't cry, pal," said Rooty. "It's just a bug, after all. There's always more."

Travis, red in the face and breathing hard, inhaled sharply through his nose, as if sucking up all the emotion and suppressing it.

"Some birthday, huh?" said Rooty.

Travis laughed, finally able to release his frustration.

"Yeah," Travis said. "One for the history books."

"Speaking of books," Rooty said with a wink. She reached into her tunic and pulled out *Wonky's Krankferten Creatures* from where she'd secured it. "Why don't you enjoy this, so you don't have to worry about racing? I'm sure there's something really weird in there that we haven't seen yet."

Travis took the book, but before he could reply, a booming sound occurred from the city walls.

GONG GONG GONG!

The Mercy Square bell echoed throughout town, stopping the orphans and all the other townspeople in their tracks. A visitor had come to Mercy Square.

The orphans rushed to the window. They could see the other villagers doing the same from the windows of their own houses and shops. This was suddenly everyone's business. A pang of fear rushed through Travis's mind. *This visitor*, Travis wondered. *Is it a friend or foe?*

A VERY STRANGE VISITOR

After a moment of fearful reluctance, the town guardsmen frantically opened the gate and saluted the visitor's carriage in a feigned attempt to seem professional, like they did this all the time, and no, of course they weren't surprised to see somebody, anybody who wished to enter their walls.

Into Mercy Square trotted a horse-drawn carriage, black and foreboding in appearance. It had ornate wheels with spindly spider-leg spokes. It looked to be a hearse of some kind. There was no driver, giving the carriage the appearance that it was driven by a ghost.

Without prompting or direction, the horse made a direct line for the orphanage and stopped outside its front stoop. It then clopped its front-left hoof twice to signal its arrival. The orphans raced downstairs to get a closer look at the carriage. When they arrived, they saw that the owner of the carriage had already entered the orphanage. He was a gigantic man, perhaps three hundred and fifty pounds, tall enough that the top of his leaf-brimmed hat scraped the ceiling. He was wearing a verdant robe tied at the waist with a sash. There were lifelike leaves emblazoned on his clothing from top to bottom.

"He's a living forest," said Travis.

As the man moved the leaves seemed to sway like branches in the wind. In facial appearance he looked to be about two hundred and seventy years old. His eyes were weary like he'd recently awoken from a life-long nap. As he blinked, he scanned the children from right to left, surveying them.

The children quieted and put their hands behind their backs so as to seem more innocent. They were beginning to think the same thing, that this man had come to adopt one of them. *This could be my chance to escape,* Travis thought. Even if it meant living with an old Tree Man, it had to be better than Mercy Square.

But a dark thought bit at Travis's lip. *What if I am adopted and forced to leave Rooty behind?* Travis believed he deserved to be adopted. *But maybe that's just a lie to make myself feel better.* No, he needed it to be true. Travis took a deep breath, tried to puff himself up to look taller, licked his palms- *blech, what a taste-* and straightened out his hair so his eyes were visible. Travis had blue eyes and sandy blonde hair and a nice smile. He had admired himself in Vonkenschtook's mirror many times, at least until Vonkenschtook had beaten him for it. If Travis were ever to meet a girl, a real girl, not a mud-covered partner-in-crime like Rooty, he would surely strike her fancy.

Yes, he told himself. *You must believe you are attractive and then maybe you will seem attractive. If you slouch like a whelp, the old Tree Man may think, 'Oh, there is an unfortunate sort, not worthy of adoption.'*

Travis hated that the world was so shallow, so judgmental based on appearances, but he had no choice but to participate in its shallowness if he had any hope of escape. So off he went, grinning and batting his eyes like a baby fawn, perhaps overacting a bit. Rooty gave him a look like she thought he had lost his mind. Travis toned it down a little, but still tried to seem as adorable as possible.

Rooty is just being competitive, I'm sure, he thought.

It wasn't long before the other orphans caught wind of this strategy and begin shuffling their feet cutely, humming fancifully, and making fools of themselves in hopes of seeming presentable.

Vonkenschtook slid between the Tree Man and the orphans and glowered at the children, whispering angrily, "Straighten up and behave like adults, not wild pixies at a jubilee!"

Everybody stopped swooning and stood up straight like soldiers. If nothing else, Vonkenschtook had at least taught them proper military posture.

"I have come to inspect your wares," said the rasping old Tree Man as he sauntered over to the stool where Vonkenschtook normally sat and slouched down upon it. As soon as his rump hit the seat his entire body seemed to melt into a lumpy pile, making him look like fallen foliage. He gestured with one hand as though even that was exhausting. "Have them approach me one-by-one for questioning."

Rooty's eyes widened. She turned to Travis. He returned the panicked expression. *I didn't know there would be a formal interview,* thought Travis. *I should have prepared a speech or a song or something. Diadra, save me! What are my positive qualities again? Oh, blast it all. What have I been doing with my life?*

"I will start with you," said the Tree Man, staring directly at Travis.

The Tree Man's eyes were like the murky depths of a forest lake. Travis could swear he almost saw ripples within them, dragonflies buzzing about their watery surface. His gaze was strange and unnerving. Travis was no longer certain he even wanted to be adopted by this man, but there was no doubt that the old man wanted to speak to him and there would be no alternative course.

"Are you certain?" asked Vonkenschtook, exasperated by the Tree Man's choice. "He is... of questionable stock, and terrible behavior."

Of course you'd say that, thought Travis.

"Do you wish to make a sale or not?" the Tree Man asked.
"Right away," Vonkenschtook said, rushing over to Travis, taking the boy by the arm and dragging him forcefully to the Tree Man.

"Do not fail me again, or I'll rid myself of you in a less pleasant way," Vonkenschtook whispered to Travis before shoving him forward.

Travis staggered toward the Tree Man, nearly tumbling onto the man's leafy gut. There seemed to be a strange warbling energy emanating from the Tree Man's robes. Travis could feel it prickling the air around him as he approached. It almost felt like that energy, whatever it was, had helped steady Travis, had kept him from tipping over at the last second. But that wasn't possible, was it?

Travis's eyes met the Tree Man's murky pools. Travis swallowed his fears, remembering that he should try to be adorable. He batted his eyelashes and smiled semi-prettily, but the Tree Man saw right through his act.

"BA-HA-HA!" bellowed the Tree Man.

The whole orphanage quivered from the force of his laughter. Travis could hear the trees outside shaking with rapturous delight.

The Tree Man tapped a fat finger against Travis's chest. "Do you take me for a fool, boy?"

Travis was uncertain. He had been trying his hardest to be adorable. Then a strange fear struck Travis. Perhaps Travis was incapable of being adorable. Perhaps his own ego had prevented him from seeing the truth, that he was hideous. Travis's breath quickened as anxiety gripped his chest like a tightening vice.

"Ch-ch-chh," The Tree Man cooed. "E'layom. Be at peace."

Travis raised his head and met the man's gaze. Was this man a Vec, an outlaw? To practice magic openly was a crime in Krankfert, but he seemed... different. Could he be so bold as to use his vectory now, in public?

"I'll remind you that my orphans are quite expensive," said Vonkenschtook. "Even the little rat-like ones like him. I train them all with expert care."

This was news to Travis, as he had been repeatedly told by Vonkenschtook that he was 'absolutely worthless.' However, in the face of a profit it seemed that Vonkenschtook was willing to bend his convictions ever so slightly.

There was something about the practical manner of Vonkenschtook's statement that seemed to ruffle the Tree Man's feathers. His leafy greens seemed to age and decay, as if transitioning from summer vibrancy into autumnal death at the drop of a hat. The Tree Man shuddered and closed his eyes, seemingly shrinking down into his own body, like a turtle's head retracting into its shell.

"Life is measured in coin is it?" The Tree Man asked.

It was clear that the Tree Man had succinctly nailed Vonkenschtook's personal philosophy. Normally Vonkenschtook might have retaliated, but instead he stayed silent, his lips twitching. He was nothing if not fervent to close the deal.

Realizing that Vonkenschtook would not defend himself from this accusation, the Tree Man flippantly gestured to his carriage outside.

"There is a sack of coin in my carriage," he murmured. "You may take anything you wish from it."

This sounded like a good enough deal to Vonkenschtook, so he immediately ran outside, leaving the children with the Tree Man and Needle, who was now standing next to the orphans with his arms behind his back and a respectable look on his face, as if he believed he might be adopted too.

"Focus your attention on me," the Tree Man said to Travis. "Answer me honestly and do not fib. I have ways of knowing."

If Vonkenschtook had made such a claim, Travis would never have believed him. But there was something about the Tree Man's murky eyes that made Travis think this bizarre claim might have some truth to it.

"Now," the Tree Man said, "what can you tell me about that orphan keeper of yours? What sort of man is he?"

Travis wanted to seem adorable, but he also did not wish to fib.

"He's, eh, he's alright, I suppose," Travis said.

"Do not fib," the Tree Man said firmly.

There was something about the Tree Man's hot, swampy breath that reminded Travis of a frog-ridden bog. He could not stand to be this close to the strange old man for much longer, so he blurted out what came immediately to mind.

"Oh, he's a horrible pompous oaf," Travis began. “He treats us like servants, barely feeds us, and he treats me worst of all. I- I hate him.”

"Ch-Chh," cooed the Tree Man. "I understand. And if you had the power, would you kill this man, Vonkenschtook?"

Travis was shocked back into silence. The Tree Man had not been surprised by Travis’s words, and now, here he was suggesting murder. Travis had never even considered such a thing. He certainly disliked Vonkenschtook, but to take the man's life? Vonkenschtook had been Travis's sole protector, even if he had been stingy and cruel. Could Travis kill anyone?

"I- I don't know," Travis said. “I don’t think so. It’s wrong, isn’t it?”

The old man stared at him cautiously, scanning him for error. After a few seconds of squinting, the Tree Man patted Travis's head.

"The story of a man’s life requires him to answer such questions. But free yourself from guilt, child. I wished only to ask your opinion. Judgment and morality are the Fates' domain. Mortal men must survive however they can.”

Travis had no idea what the old man was saying, but it sounded intoxicating, like he'd been waiting to hear such strange philosophy his entire life. He'd been sinking in quicksand, and the Tree Man had thrown him a vine. Travis wanted to learn what this man had to teach him about the world. It felt like this man had come from the wilderness to save Travis, to redeem him from his sorry lot in life.

"I have made my decision," said the Tree Man.

Vonkenschtook had only just re-entered the orphanage, arms full of coins from the Tree Man's carriage. The Tree Man did not turn his head to speak to him, as if he could see the room clearly without even using his eyes.

Mildly startled by the Tree Man's omniscience, Vonkenschtook dropped a few of the coins. While forcing an appreciative smile, Vonkenschtook kicked the dropped coins into a small pile before him as he walked so that he could reclaim them later, making sure to eye the orphans villainously while doing so, warning them to keep away from his loot.

Travis felt certain that he was about to be adopted. His heart began beating so quickly it felt like it might burst free from his ribs and scamper out the door. This was the moment he'd long been waiting for!

"This one," the Tree Man said, patting Travis's head, "is a disappointment. I shall instead take the other filthy child and be on my way."

Travis followed the Tree Man's finger. He was pointing squarely at Rooty.

THE CLEVER BUG

Shame and sorrow washed over Travis in waves. The Tree Man had rejected him. It was Rooty that he wanted. Short Rooty, younger Rooty, tick-ridden Rooty! And not only had Travis been rejected, this decision meant that Rooty, his best and only friend was leaving him! It was like a nightmare. Worst of all, it was yet another slight on the worst birthday imaginable. How had this all gone so horribly wrong?

The Tree Man took Rooty by the shoulder and ushered her outside to his carriage.

"Travis," Rooty called. "I'll always remember you! Take care of you-know-what!"

Travis did not understand what she meant until Rooty was already inside the carriage. The Tree Man's horse bowed graciously and lead the carriage back out through the gates of Mercy Square. The guards slammed the gates shut behind the carriage as it rode away. It suddenly occurred to Travis in the throes of all this emotional upheaval that Rooty had been referring to their book, that shared prized-possession. *But what difference does it matter now that you're gone? You're off to a world of adventure. Who knows what things you'll see? All I have are words and pictures.*

"Well, that's one out of two bad apples," Vonkenschtook said, shrugging and sighing. "Looks like you're all alone now."

He smirked at Travis before going to count his coins. The orphans followed Vonkenschtook and Travis wandered lifelessly behind them, a phantom.

"Quite the haul, Needle," Vonkenschtook said, inspecting each coin lovingly.

Needle whistled approvingly. Travis's stomach turned. To have his best friend reduced to a pile of coins, to have his one defender sold off to a stranger, leaving him to suffer Vonkenschtook's constant torment- it was too much.

Travis groaned loudly, turning the heads of everyone in the room. He rushed back upstairs and burst into the shared bedroom, flinging himself onto his sleep-sack.

Ruined, Travis thought. *My whole life is ruined.*

He'd been robbed of the plate, his racing bug, and his best friend all on the same lousy birthday. Rooty was probably already on some exciting adventure with the Tree Man. Travis pressed his face against the straw mat and muffled a scream.

He could hear the others cheering downstairs, like they were celebrating the fiscal boon, or perhaps throwing a birthday party for everyone who wasn't Travis.

Travis compulsively jutted his hands into the place where the rotting wood made a small hole in the corner of the room and after a moment of frantically clawing, he reached the book, *Wonky's Krankferten Monsters*, which he had hidden there.

He brushed dust and spider webbing off of the cover, and he admired the glimmering gilding on the title letters, which shimmered well in the daylight, even obscured by the cool grey clouds that coated the sky. He just wanted to close his eyes and disappear. He tried to force himself into slumber, allowing the exhaustion of the emotional experience to carry him deeper and deeper into his imagination, where nothing real could ever harm him. His consciousness faded, until he suddenly became aware of a noise coming from the windowsill.

Skitter-skitter-skitter.

Travis perked his head up suddenly. How long had he been asleep? No one was back yet, so it couldn't have been too long. *Yes,* he realized. He was by himself. And he knew that sound.

It was the sound of a ricktick clattering its way across the windowsill nearest to Travis. It was a big fat one too. Travis instantly decided that if anything was going to salvage this awful day, winning the Ricktick Rumble might just do it. *But was there even a reason to race anymore?* Rooty ran the races, and Rooty was gone. Travis sighed deeply, tried his best to remain manly while curled in the fetal position, and stifled the sobs he wanted to emit. If the other children should catch wind of his sorrow, he'd likely be pummeled all over again. He had no friend to protect him, no hope for the future.

Skitter-skitter-skitter.

It was scuttling down the wall now. It seemed to be heading in his direction slowly, timidly. Travis readied himself. He sat up then twisted onto his knees and crouched, like a kitten ready to pounce. Just as the ricktick was within range, he inhaled sharply and leapt toward it.

"I say," cried the bug, startling Travis into an awkward tumble.

Rather than clasping the bug in his palms like he'd planned,

Travis skidded his palms on the splintering floorboards and rolled over, trying not to squish it. *What in the Fate's domain is happening?* He wondered, now scrambling backward from the bug on his buttocks. Once he was safely a few feet away from it, his chest heaving with fright, he tried to make sense of things. *Was it Gulken playing a prank?* But there was no one else in the bedroom, and the voice had sounded rather posh, not at all like Gulken's mix of groans and donkey-like braying.

"I say," repeated the ricktick. "Were you planning to squish me? I toddle all the way up this hideous building and that's how you repay me?"

"But- but!" Travis was too confused to speak clearly.

"No, no," replied the ricktick. "It's pronounced *BUG*. Hmm, perhaps all this time away from your family has resulted in some form of brain damage. I wouldn't be surprised if whoever ran this garbage pile of an orphanage was feeding you swamp water and slugs. Why look at you! You haven't a scrap of fat on your body, but, my *word!* Your eyes! How splendidly they reflect your mother's countenance! And your jawline, now that's clearly your father's, maybe a bit of the shoulders as well. Yes, Travis, you're the spitting image of both of them, well, half-and-half."

Travis scrambled backward against the wall, trying to distance himself from this bizarre creature. *How is it talking?* He wondered. *And how does it know my name? Why is it speaking about my parents? Is this bug a Vec? Have I lost my mind?*

"Why, Travis Sebastian!" called the bug. "It's rude not to respond to a guest, especially one who's gone through such trouble to find you. I suppose I could keep talking if you're really that dumbstruck. I happen to enjoy waxing poetic, although these particular surroundings do little to inspire one's creativity."

The bug had spoken Travis's last name, Sebastian, as if it were common knowledge, but Travis was certain he had not heard that name since his parents had died. How could a bug come by such privileged information?
"Vec!" Travis cried out. "It's vectory!"

The others were too consumed with celebrating Vonkenschtook's newfound riches to pay much attention to Travis's cries from upstairs. Needle was slapping his knees percussively while Vonkenschtook hummed and danced with his coins. The orphans watched with a mixture of confusion and amusement.

"Hush now, Travis," the bug whispered. "You must not reveal me to anyone. I'm here on, eh, a secret mission of sorts. For the royal family. Yes, that's the sort of thing you children enjoy, isn't it? Yes, so calm down and listen to my tale. I'm sure you'll find my adventures most exhilarating."

"Why are you a bug?" asked Travis. "What sort of bug works for the royal family? Are you a spy or an evil witch-man?"

"Heavens," said the bug. "I expected you to be a bit less trepidatious and mildly more excited to see me. I mean to rescue you, of course! Well, not now in my current form. I couldn't carry you out of here with these meager appendages, now could I? But if you'll keep me safe and sound, I'm sure we'll be able to abscond with you in a few days' time. Isn't that right, Betsy?"

The bug turned to its right, where no one was standing, and cooed as if stroking a pet lovingly. "Yes," the bug said. "You're anxious to meet Travis too, aren't you?"

"You're mad," said Travis. "Or I'm mad. One thing is for certain, and that's one of us is mad. And I'd rather not lose my mind on my birthday!"

"Birthday?" the bug exclaimed, hopping happily toward him. "Well congratulations, boy! And how fortuitous for me to arrive now."

"Get out of here," said Travis. "I don't want to get mixed up with some vector-using outlaw. My life is a prison already."

The bug stopped getting carried away with its own enthusiasm and wiggled its antennae towards Travis's face as if trying to read his emotions clearly. "Yes," it said. "I see. You've suffered greatly here, haven't you? Apologies. I thought you might be safe amongst such rural greenery, but I suppose evil rears its head in all places. We must take greater caution to protect you."

"I don't want or need your help," Travis said, though he wasn't entirely certain this was true. He only knew that he felt emotionally exhausted, and could not tolerate any more of this insanity.

"I did not wish for you to suffer," said the bug. "I do apologize. You were smuggled from your parents' home under great duress, as you were wanted by the Queen for execution. I'm sure most of that nonsense is cleared up by now, at least I hope so. The Princess is on your side."

This last bit woke Travis from the foulness of his mood.

"The Princess?" Travis asked, eyes suddenly brightening.

"Oh, that's the part that struck your fancy, was it?" The bug asked. " I see you're as keen to meet her as she is to meet you. There is much we have to discuss."

The bug grasped ahold of a small stone lodged between two of the floorboards, plucked it free, and sat atop it, crossing two of its legs like a human being.

"You aren't really a bug, are you?" Travis asked.

"You may call me Kane Verdalea," said the bug. "I am a friend of your family and the royal family, although the two families are not particularly fond of one another since the tragic fire."

The fire, Travis thought. He could feel the flames on his face. *This bug knows about it too. My memories- perhaps he can tell me more.*

"Right," said the bug. "Here's what's important. Due to a sort of uh, disagreement between your parents and the king, your home was burned to a crisp. You were hidden away by a family friend, apparently in this dismal place. The trouble was, you were hidden so well that no one knew quite where to find you. The man who hid you, well, he was killed, and so the secret died with him. I've searched for you for years, and here you are, by the Fates' divine will!"

This news was all so strange, and yet it fit so cleanly with the scraps of memory in Travis's mind. He could see his father erupting in fire, almost as if the fire were a part of his own body. He could see his mother's face, frozen in fear, as a blade came toward her. She was reaching out to grasp it, sacrificing her hand. His father was trying to kill the assailant with a fire of his own making. But a mortal man could not create fire from inside himself. That would mean...

"Was my father a Vec?!" Travis asked.

"No," the bug laughed. "Your father was much too powerful to be a Vec in the normal sense. No, if anything he was the halfway point between a human and a Fate. He was not like any creature I have ever known, or likely will ever know. Travis, your father, was one of the last remaining Elementals in the world."

From the sound of the bug's timbre, this was apparently quite the achievement, but Travis was still grappling with the implication that his dear old departed dad was some sort of magical criminal. He sputtered a bit then finally spoke.

"You mean he was a fugitive! And the royals wanted him dead! Oh, Fates help me! No wonder Vonkenschtook hates me. I'm the son of a criminal!"

Kane the bug huffed with exasperation.

"How dare you disrespect your father's memory with such tedious accusations! The laws of mortal men were made to oppress magical beings, and can only be understood as acts of fear and betrayal, not the justice of the righteous." The bug stood and began waving its limbs wildly while ranting, almost acting like a thumb-sized Vonkenschtook. "I'd heard tell of the lack of schooling in these parts, but the fact you're unaware of the monumentality of being the son of an Elemental is absolutely baffling! Don't you see what power lies dormant inside of you?"

Travis had not even considered the implications for himself.

"Does that mean," Travis gulped. "I could become- oh, Karol's madness..."

"Yes," the bug stated plainly. "You could be a Vec above Vecs! One mightier than any, capable of such magical feats that the world might cheer with amazement, that is, if we lived someplace where such acts weren't illegal."

"I'm a criminal," said Travis. "And I didn't even do anything."

"Oh, it's not all bad if you keep it secret," Kane the bug said. Then noticing the tome at Travis's hip, the bug exclaimed. "I say! Is that a copy of *Wonky's*? That shall suit our purposes nicely for the time being. Let's see here."

Kane the bug scampered over to the pages of the book and began to kick them open rapidly in a singular direction, flitting through page after page of mythical beasts. He stopped on a page covered with archaic runes and symbols. It showed a blue humanoid figure floating in mid-air with a serene expression and a distinct lack of pupils. There were purple swirls that wrapped the creature's flesh like vines. Travis saw that the pages were littered with warnings of the creature's dangerous abilities and otherworldly power.

"That's my dad?" gasped Travis. "Frankly I don't see the resemblance!"

Kane the bug laughed.

"Well, your full potential is yet to be unleashed, isn't it?" he explained. "That's part of the reason I'm here. To help you understand your abilities."

"I don't want to be all blue and floaty," said Travis. "I like being a normal human, just the way I am. I wish you'd never told me any of this!"

"I understand the shock this all must be, but let's try to keep this meeting celebratory, shall we?" said Kane. "Do you know how long it's taken me to track you down? Travis? Don't you turn your back on me."

Travis slumped back toward the wall onto his sleep-sack, while the bug flailed wildly, trying to get his attention.

"We need to get you out of this dreadful orphanage as quickly as possible. I can almost hear the floorboards breaking beneath us-

or, say, what's *that* sound?"

"Oh no," Travis said.

Travis scooped the bug into his palms just as he heard the other children barreling down the hallway and into the bedroom. If they discovered the truth about him, there would be no doubt that Vonkenschtook would have him hanged in the street.

THE LITTLE LOUDMOUTH

"Let me go," the bug said, struggling a bit, then recognizing the reason for the noise, wiggled his antennae and said, "Oh, I see. Hush now, boy."

Travis clutched the bug tightly against his chest and hoped like mad that the others wouldn't notice him doing so. Then, pressing the bug against him with one hand, Travis took *Wonky's Krankferten Monsters* and tossed it as hard as he could out the window, where by luck or some vectory, it landed neatly in a bush outside.

BOOM. The door burst open. Gulken and the others entered the room.

Gulken stopped directly in front of Travis. Travis winced in anticipation of another bug murder. But Gulken was too preoccupied to pay Travis any additional mind.

"Quiet down! Now quickly! Set it up," he said.

The children constructed the ricktick racetrack with bubbling excitement. It dawned on Travis that even without Rooty, the progenitor of the game, the orphans were still planning on conducting a bug race. This seemed sacrilegious to Travis, as Rooty was no longer there to enjoy the festivities. *How could they be so callous as to treat her like nothing? How could Gulken suddenly take control of the whole thing as if it were his?* But there the orphans were, pawing over Rooty's belongings, building the racetrack as she'd taught them.

"What are you doing?" Travis shouted, unable to restrain himself. "That's Rooty's racetrack! You think it belongs to you now that she's gone? Shame on you!"

The children stopped. In all the excitement of planning the race, they'd forgotten about Travis. This was indeed a bit awkward.

"Shut it, whelp," Gulken spat. "You don't got a bug, so your opinion don't matter."

Gulken grinned widely, his teeth pointing in all sorts of directions. Some of the other orphans chuckled and nodded, then went back to work on the track.

Furter and Crump, the two eldest orphans and de facto leaders of the group, came up alongside Gulken. Furter looked like a scarecrow that had been stretched uncomfortably taut and Crump resembled a werewolf in training, having copious amounts of body hair, especially along his arms.

"Don't take it too hard," said Furter, slapping a palm on Travis's shoulder.

"A'course it's sad that Rooty's gone," said Crump. "But we got something to celebrate all the same. Take a gander at this!"

He held up a gold coin, one of the many that Vonkenschtook had received as payment for Rooty. Travis was shocked that Vonkenschtook had somehow forgotten to collect every last coin.

"It fell between the floorboards," said Furter. "I saw it go down there, squeezed my way in, and swiped it! Got a few snapworm bites, but Vonk's none the wiser!"

Furter showed off a few scratches on his fingers where the snapworms had scratched him, then pocketed the coin again, smiling with pride.

Kane the bug wriggled his way through Travis's fingers and spoke up. "Ah, I see your cronies are the thieving type. Normally I might be offended but given our current predicament, I hope they've taught you a thing or two."

The other boys stared at Travis's hands as if they'd heard Kane speaking. Travis froze with fear, then subtly tried to cover the bug's mouth.

"You got another bug? No fair," said Gulken.

"Well then," said Furter, "It looks like Travis can race too!"

"Competition is heating up!" said Crump. "Your bug is clicking and hissing like it's raring to go."

Travis tilted his head with confusion.

"You mean, you can't hear it talking?" Travis asked.

Sensing the earnestness of Travis's question, the other boys exchanged a look that suggested they thought he was losing his mind. Not wanting to rattle his nerves even further, Furter patted him on the shoulder again.

"Uh, well sure we do," Furter said with a mix of condescension and pity. "What a lovely speaking voice he has, Travis. Yep, who even needs Rooty with a fine, uh, talking bug like that."

Furter rejoined the other boys as they walked away to inspect the track.

"Poor kid," said Crump. "He's lost his mind from sadness. Can't say I blame him. But he'll be way easier to beat this way!"

Gulken and Crump began arguing about who had the stronger racing insect. Travis was left alone again, clasping his ricktick, confused as to what had just transpired.

"Don't worry, Travis," said Kane the bug. "If my vectory has gone as planned, they should only hear the buzzing of a regular ricktick. We can converse, and they'll be none the wiser."

"So Furter was only being nice to me because he thinks I'm crazy."

"Quite," said Kane. "A perfect alibi. Every time you speak to me your insanity will be further revealed to the boys around you, thereby solidifying it."

Travis began shaking the bug angrily.

"You said you were going to help me," Travis growled, "not make me look insane! I'm perfectly sane! Why can't you make me seem normal?!"

This was when Travis noticed that the other orphans were staring at him as he seemed to be having a full conversation with the ricktick in his hands. Some giggled, while others just shook their heads and rolled their eyes wearily, as if to say, new day, same old Travis.

"Excellent acting," said Kane. "They're sure to underestimate you now. Why you nearly had me convinced that you were actually enraged!"

"Oy, Travis," called Crump. "Why don't you talk to some of us humans for a change. It might help calm you down a little." He gestured for Travis to join the rest of the orphans at the starting line of the racetrack.

Travis took a deep breath and walked over, trying to smile as sanely as possible. This did not put anyone at ease. His skin felt prickly as everyone eyed him.

Gulken reached forward and clasped his hands atop Travis's once more, putting pressure onto Kane, the clever bug, making him cry out with fear.

"I oughta squish this one too," said Gulken.

"Hang on, Gulken," said Furter, shoving Gulken away from Travis, just before the weight of his hands became too much for Kane or Travis to bear. "You can't go around squishing the other racers or we'll have set the whole track up for nothing."

Travis breathed a sigh of relief as Gulken stopped seething to consider this, putting his index finger between his lips and sucking it thoughtfully.

Crump elbowed Gulken gently in the side and whispered loudly enough for everyone to hear that Travis "was already losing his marbles after what happened with Rooty," suggesting that it was best not to push him any further off the deep end, for fear of what he might do once his last shred of sanity had depleted.

Gulken chuckled a little, as if picturing a frazzled and twitching Travis in his mind, then raised his palms upward, sucked some air in his nose, and turned back to the track. This was apparently an act of absolution, at least for the time being. Travis could feel his anxiety releasing its icy grip. *They're going to let me race.*

"I say," said Kane, the clever bug, "that Gulken there is quite the brute! If he attempts to squish me again, I may have to squish him in person. Not that I'm the sort who would actually harm a child, but you know, when one is small and fragile it becomes that much easier to hold a grudge."

Furter laughed at the clicking and hissing he heard from Travis's insect. "He's a funny one," said Furter. "Talks almost as much as Vonkenschtook."

"And he makes just as much sense," added Crump.

The two boys tilted their heads back and guffawed at their own cleverness. Gulken grumbled, still unwilling to associate Travis with merriment in any form.

"Enough talky-talk," Gulken said. "Let's race. I want to win that gold coin so I can buy myself a meal worthy of a king."

A gold coin could fetch a fine meal from the butcher, enough for Gulken and whoever else he wanted to share it with, although knowing Gulken that was likely nobody. Travis had never tasted ham, but he could imagine its savory splendor melting in his mouth along with berry juice and fresh baked bread.

"Well if we win," said Crump, gesturing to himself and Furter, "we're going to ask the blacksmith to make us a sword, one so strong it can slice up a billion jarters."

Furter and Crump began mock sword-fighting with invisible blades. A few of the younger orphans began to clap and cheer joyously.

Once Furter had Crump in a headlock, Furter turned to Travis casually and asked him what *he* would do if he somehow managed to get the gold coin.

Without hesitating, Travis replied, “Bribe a guard, get outside the walls, and head for the Clockwork City. I want to see it with my own eyes. Then after that, I want to see the whole world. There’s got to be someplace better than here.”

Gulken clucked his tongue dismissively. “Always acting better than us,” he said. “Even though you’ve got no chance of winning! My Gertrude will make mincemeat of any bug you race, easily!”

Gulken reached into his pocket and scrounged up a thick black beetle. This was apparently Gertrude, Gulken's bug, one he'd been hiding away for just such an occasion. To Travis, Gertrude seemed formidable, but he wondered if her thick outer shell allowed her much maneuverability on the track.

"Don't be so confident," said Crump, slipping his way free from Furter, finally. “You’ll have to deal with little Corny as well.”

Crump reached into his short-pants and procured a thin light-brown insect, about half the size of Gertrude. Travis immediately recognized this as a young ricktick, maybe a month old. *He’s taking a risk on that one,* Travis thought, eyeing the way the young bug darted around Crump’s palm excitedly. Crump could barely keep the little thing contained with both hands. If it was sufficiently motivated by food, there would no doubt that this bug could be a threat, given its penchant for quick acceleration. But young bugs had other downsides. It was well-known that young bugs had difficulty focusing on any particular task, as they would often get distracted by loud noises or shiny objects.

“Yep,” said Furter, grabbing the little bug as it tried to leap away.

"His name's Cornelius, but we call him Corny for short, on account of Crump can't pronounce Cornelius."

"I can so pronounce Corni- Corniverous," said Crump.

Travis then realized that he had not discussed the concept of the race with Kane. *Even if the little loudmouth agrees*, Travis thought, *who's to say he'll be speedy? I'm going to need to be mighty persuasive, or be stuck within these walls forever.*

"I'll need a moment before we begin to encourage my racer," Travis said, turning his back to the others just fast enough to avoid noticing their disturbed looks and confusion. Once he was outside of earshot, he whispered into his hands.

"Listen you," he began. "I don't know if you're really a Vec or a bug who learned a bunch of big words at university, but you're going to race for me. I need that gold coin so I can leave this horrid place. If you help me, I'll... I'll get you all the dragonfly eggs you can eat. How does that sound?"

"Blech," said Kane, shaking his arms in disgust. "A fine steak would be a far better incentive, don't you think?"

"I can't afford steak *and* to bribe the guards," Travis shouted at the bug while the others watched, dumbfounded. Then, lowering his voice, and clearing his throat a little to try and maintain some dignity, he begged. "Please, you must do this for me, and then I'll do whatever you wish. Can't we strike a deal?"

"Oh, alright," said Kane. "I'll run your silly race if it really is your birthday and all. I suppose I did show up to these festivities a bit empty-handed, or whatever these spiky things on the ends of my legs are. A standard point A to point B affair, I imagine? Nothing too strenuous, Fates save me. I did expend a lot of energy just climbing up those slippery walls out there."

Kane began doing strange calisthenics and stretches in Travis's hand. To try to focus him on the task ahead, Travis aimed Kane from the starting line to the finish, noting each obstacle along the way.

"I say," Kane exclaimed. "Is it really necessary that the track is so dangerous? You know I'm beginning to think this may be a bad idea. How can I protect you if I'm eaten by snapworms? Yes, I'm certain we both agree that this race is out of the question. Why don't you remain content in listening to my fascinating stories for the evening? Then in a few days' time we can reassess our escape plans."

Travis's nose scrunched up like a bunny rabbit's. His head began vibrating with anger. "No!" Travis cried. "This is my birthday wish, you stupid bug! It's now or never. Besides, you've already agreed! There's no backing out now!"

Having heard this last outburst as well, Gulken chimed in with another jab. "You hear that, boys? Travis's bug is as chicken as he is!" Gulken began imitating a chicken and prancing about in mimicry of Travis, somehow making himself look stupider than Travis had at any point that day.

"Oh, what an oaf," Kane said. "Fine, you spoiled boy. I'll race." After a lengthy, overdramatic sigh, Kane gave a salute and stood at attention, signaling that he was ready for duty.

"Thank you," said Travis. "Whatever you like to eat, we'll find it later."

Travis practically skipped with glee as he returned to the starting line.

"Yes," Kane said, "well, that's very generous, but as I've told you,

I am a very human-ish Vec in reality, so I eat most things that anyone eats! Toffees, chocolate cake, roasted boar with beans and gravy, copious amounts of wine..."

Travis plopped Kane down at the starting line next to his competition. Kane stopped babbling about food once he caught scent of the two bugs to his left, who were both inspecting him and trying to climb atop him immediately.

"I say," Kane shouted. "This is no way to greet the competition. Unhand me, you vile stink beetles! I am not one of your kin! Oh, why did I have to be as attractive an insect as I am in my natural form?"

Crump separated the insects and lined them up, snapping his fingers to try to keep Cornelius from getting distracted or running away. As Travis watched Crump struggle to direct his bug, Travis realized his one advantage. Kane could understand him, while the other bugs had no idea what their owners were saying.

"What's that bug of yours called anyway?" Crump asked Travis.

"For our purposes," Kane interjected, "it is best not to reveal my true name. Instead invent a pseudonym. Something simple that a child might naturally concoct."

"His name is Loudmouth," Travis replied.

"How dare you?" the newly dubbed Loudmouth cried. "After all the effort I've put into hoofing this insect over here and finding you, you give me the most insulting name you could muster up? This is an absolute outrage, and I won't..."

The bug continued babbling at Travis while the other orphans listened to its clicking and hissing. Furter nodded in acknowledgement of the name.

"Yep," said Furter. "It's a sure fit. He won't shut up for a second."

The little Loudmouth stopped sputtering at Travis and turned his berating to Furter.

"Now see here, you gangly scarecrow of a child," Kane spat. "I won't be castigated by such a sallow malcontent. I can stop talking any time I feel like!"

Kane tried to hold his tongue for a second as if to prove this, but immediately started clicking and hissing again.

"The fact remains that I simply will not give you the satisfaction of controlling me," he continued. "That is the only reason I continue speaking, and not because your half-witted satire has any basis in reality."

The other orphans chuckled with delight at what looked to be a ricktick giving the comparatively enormous Furter a piece of its mind. Furter had enough sense as to know when to play along for the public's delight.

"What's that ya say?" he asked Kane. "You're mad you ain't got a girlfriend? Well don't take it out on me that your face looks like that."

The children guffawed and howled at this riotous routine. Furter smiled smugly, having improvised a satisfactory joke for his peers. Kane was still sputtering, but sounded to Travis as if he'd actually been caught off guard by this latest jape.

"G- girlfriend?" Kane said, his voice faltering slightly. "I could have many a girlfriend if I wanted one! Well, that would be caddish. I'm no cad, you see. I'm a one woman or uh, insect, kind of man! I just happen to be so devoted to Travis at present that I couldn't possibly focus on romance!"

Kane turned to Travis for support on this issue, but Travis waved the bug away.

"Don't look at me, Loudmouth," Travis said. "You started this argument."

Now Kane the Loudmouth was acting sullen, hunched over as best a bug could, kicking the floorboards with pent-up aggression.

"Travis is his bug's girlfriend," Gulken said.

"Alright, alright," said Furter. "Let's save the fighting for the race."

Furter and Crump began ordering the orphans to prep the food for the track. Flowery bits, buds and leaves and petals, were placed at increments along the track as incentive for the bugs to keep moving forward.

"Oy, hang on," said Crump. "We got a whole bunch of dead ones here."

There were a bunch of dead rickticks on the underside of one of the broken pots that made up Storm Mountain Pass. Crump shook them out of the bottom of the broken pot while the younger children gathered around to collect the dead bugs and feast upon them like roasted potato slices.

Kane the clever bug watched this gluttony with horror.

"They mean to kill me and eat me, Travis!" he screamed. "We must escape!"

"Don't worry," Travis whispered while the other children were gorging. "I can tell you where the deadly parts are."

"How many deadly parts are there?!" Loudmouth was once again living up to his name, pacing and shouting before the starting line while Cornelius and Gertrude watched him with great interest. "No, no, Travis. This won't do at all. I won't have anything happen to this bug after I've taken such great strides in projecting my aura inside of him. This race is but a trifle compared to the importance of our larger mission. We must avoid it at all costs."

"Alright," said Furter. "Looks like we're ready to begin."

"It's too late," Travis whispered. "We're about to start. Don't panic. It will only make you more likely to be crushed or eaten."

"Ready your Rickticks," said Crump. "The winner of this race wins the gold coin we took from Vonkenschtook. Remember, snitches are jarter bait."

"All betting will cease," said Furter, "in fifteen seconds!"

Suddenly orphans began betting odds and bobbins, buttons, a bloody bone, a doll head, and one turnip. Crump took stock of everything, carefully memorizing who bet what and arranging the piles accordingly. He nodded as if everything was in order and took a stance above the bugs at the starting line.

"Here we go, Mercy Square," Crump said. "Let's Ricktick Rumble!"

RICKTICK RUMBLE

Crump threw a handful of flower petals in front of the starting line. Cornelius barreled forward, getting a head start on Gertrude and Loudmouth. Gertrude, seeing Cornelius head hurriedly in one direction, followed suit. Only Loudmouth sat behind at the race track, befuddled by what was happening.

"Oh, have we started already?" Kane asked, clearly feigning confusion. "I suppose I've already lost, haven't I? Best to sit this one out and let the others race."

Travis, unsupportive of Kane's continued cowardice, flicked him forward with his finger, launching him over the starting line.

"No!" Kane cried, as the other children laughed.

Cornelius and Gertrude were nearing the upturned broom's bristling top, though Cornelius had stopped a few times while crawling up, either out of distraction or fear. Gertrude was right behind Cornelius now, getting her stride and confidently planning to overtake the younger bug. Loudmouth, on the other hand, was timidly kicking the end of the broom, testing to see if it could support his weight.

"Seems a bit un-sturdy," Loudmouth said.

The other rickticks were crawling up a leafy trail into the crude drawing of Vonkenschtook. They were headed right for the hole in Vonkenschtook's mouth.

"Move your buggy butt," said Travis. "We're going to lose!"

"I have no energy," Kane replied. "I'm simply famished from all this travel. Perhaps if you'd fed me first-"

"There's food on the track," Travis said. "But there won't be any left if you let the other bugs gobble it up first!"

Furter and Crump were cheering Cornelius on as he shot through Vonkenschtook's mouth and out the other side of the drawing.

Loudmouth's antennae wiggled.

"Why yes," Loudmouth said. "There does seem to be food near here. Mm- flower buds! Yes! I must have them! I must, I must! My buggy belly craves it!"

With a sudden burst of electric speed, Loudmouth began racing up the broom, kicking up a tumbleweed of dust motes behind him.

"Here I was denying the bug its instincts so I could rein its movements," Kane said. "But its natural motive is for survival!"

While he was babbling Loudmouth zoomed through the mouth hole, knocking Gertrude out the other side. Gertrude was stunned and began scuttling around in circles, unsure of which way to go, acting a bit like a dog chasing its tail.

"That's not fair," Gulken said. "His bug is as crazy as he is!"

Gulken looked as though he wanted to leap atop Travis and choke him to death. Travis smiled sheepishly and shrugged, hoping he could defuse this conflict.

Loudmouth was now neck-in-neck with Cornelius as the two entered the array of broken clay pots that constituted Storm Mountain Pass. Loudmouth was trying to weasel his way past Cornelius, but the pass was tight and there wasn't much room to squeeze through. In the center of the pass was a flower bud, a delicious bug-sized treat, one that Kane's buggy belly could not resist.

"There," Loudmouth cried. "The food, the food! By the Fates I must have it!"

But Cornelius was clogging the pass. Loudmouth tried climbing along the broken vases, but he couldn't find footing.

"Yeech," Loudmouth said. "Too slippery. Why won't this squirrelly little insect move out of the way?"

In a rage Loudmouth wriggled himself underneath the lightweight Cornelius and flipped the young bug up in the air behind him. Cornelius landed upside-down and began flailing his legs in the air wildly, as if still running.

"Ah-hah!" cried Kane, closing in on the food.

Realizing he was no longer making contact with the ground, Cornelius righted himself and leapt upon Loudmouth like a jungle cat! But rather than biting his opponent, Cornelius merely clung to Loudmouth, riding him like a horse.

"What's this?" asked Kane. "Oh-ho-ho-no! I will not wear a fool for a hat."

But despite his best efforts, Kane could not flick Cornelius from his hide. The little bug was gripping Loudmouth's carapace with all its might.

"Your affection is entirely one-sided, you sticky fool," Kane complained.

"Ignore him," Travis said. "He's trying to distract you!"

Furter was hooting and hollering for Cornelius to break ahead.

"Then I must use my might!" Kane roared.
Loudmouth did an awkward somersault and flipped Cornelius off of his body. Cornelius flew forward, landing neatly on the delicious flower bud in front of them. He began hugging and nibbling it lovingly.

"No," Loudmouth said. "That's my lunch!"

Loudmouth charged forward, knocking the bud out of Cornelius's mouth. Cornelius had been mid-munch and was now entirely unhappy. The two bugs began to wrestle, pulling the food back and forth.

"This insect is the only creature on the planet more stubborn than you are, Travis!" said Kane.

"You're the one wrestling with him," said Travis. "Just focus on the finish line, would you?"

While the two bugs were wrestling over the food, Cornelius accidentally kicked the flower bud away from both of them. Just as it rolled out of reach, Gertrude came charging in and snatched it, devouring the bud in two bites. Off Gertrude went on her merry way, while Loudmouth and Cornelius were left in the dust.

"That despicable thief!" Loudmouth said.

"There's more food ahead," Travis said. "You can still win!"

"This is about more than food now, Travis," Loudmouth declared, charging onward. "This is about decency! This is about honor! This is about justice for insects everywhere!"

Travis wasn't sure what Kane meant by that, but he cheered as the little Loudmouth raced ahead. The big bug Gertrude was heading toward The Sunken Temple now, represented by a cord of rope strung across a bucket of water. It was notorious as a place where several bugs had fallen, drowning in the water below.

Gulken was shouting for his sweet Gertrude to cross the rope bridge, but Gertrude looked uncharacteristically timid when she reached the rim of the bucket. She was not as nimble as the other bugs, it seemed. As a heftier insect there was more danger that she might lose her balance along the cord and plummet to her death.

Before Gertrude could find her courage, down came Loudmouth barging toward the bucket. Cornelius had leapt atop Loudmouth once more, and was riding him like a surfboard. Kane could sense the trepidation in Cornelius's wobbly legs. Corny was scuttling around on Loudmouth's back rather than clinging firmly. Noticing this advantage, Loudmouth flicked his hindquarters upward in the air, launching Cornelius forward toward the bucket. Corny flailed madly as he soared, but rather than plunking neatly into the water, Cornelius made a mad grab for Gertrude and fixed himself to her back instead.

Gertrude was shocked by this sudden pounce, and in her fright she toppled over the side of the rope into the water below. Cornelius, still atop Gertrude even as she fell, ran around her like a rolling log to stay out of the water, while Gertrude gurgled and sputtered, flustered and unable to breathe.

"Gertrude," Gulken cried. His eyes looked like they might pop from their sockets.

Too wrapped up in his competitive fury (or perhaps ravenous hunger) the little Loudmouth scurried across the rope to the other end of the bucket, not stopping to dwell on the tragic events below. The only obstacle remaining between Loudmouth and the finish line now was that snapworm infested tree branch.

“I’ve done it,” Kane’s voice bellowed in Travis’s mind. “I’ve won the race!”

Before Travis could remind Kane of the hidden threat ahead, the clever bug was already charging along the branch. Like trees suddenly sprouting from the dirt, tall thin snapworms shot upright from holes in the branch. They began dancing menacingly, making it harder to predict their movement. Their twisting and writhing felt like the taunt of a sore winner.

“Egad!” Kane yelped. “I’m surrounded by vipers!”

THWACK! THWACK! The snapworms latched onto him, corroding his protective carapace with their acidic bites. Kane howled in horror.

“Travis!" Loudmouth shouted. "You must intercede! They're burning right through me! This ricktick will not survive much longer!”

Travis wanted to reach out and save his ricktick, but it was strictly against the rules to interfere once a bug had crossed the starting line. He did not wish for the bug to die. Who knew what sort of havoc that might wreak on the Vec controlling it? But he could not risk losing the coin. His bug had made it furthest after all.

Kane sizzled and howled as the snapworms bit into him over and over.

"This is why I didn't want to run the bloody race," Kane the Loudmouth moaned.

But Travis and his talking ricktick had underestimated one aspect of the competition, the relentless persistence of Cornelius. They had thought him a goner. He had been perched atop the dying Gertrude, bobbing at the water's surface. But with one last-ditch effort, Cornelius sprang from Gertrude's corpse to the bucket rim, pulling himself to safety and racing after Loudmouth. Now he was approaching the snapworm branch. With Loudmouth keeping the snapworms occupied, it would be easy enough for the nimble Cornelius to leap past Loudmouth and reach the finish line.

What happened next was a surprise to all involved. Cornelius, lacking the experience to recognize the deadly stakes of the race, compulsively leapt atop Loudmouth once more. Little of Loudmouth's shell was exposed due to the attachment of the snapworms, and so Cornelius bounced off the snapworms' backs and sprang a bit further down the branch.

Surprised by the sudden impact, the two snapworms detached from Loudmouth's back and began fighting amongst themselves, each blaming the other for the strike. Though sizzling and disoriented, Kane the Loudmouth found himself free from his attackers. Stumbling forward, he made his way out of their reach.

"Go Corny, go!" Furter and Crump chanted.

Cornelius was poised to succeed, but his youthful exuberance made him vibrate with excitement. Cornelius performed a playful dance for Loudmouth, shaking his rump this way and that, making little hops on the end of the branch. Furter and Crump began howling for Cornelius to stop gloating and cross the finish line.

"Out of the way, you lout," Kane said in a wobbly tone.

In a flash Cornelius gained all the knowledge that the Fate Hilauria would ever bestow upon him. At the end of the branch, an inch behind him, one final snapworm swiftly emerged and struck Cornelius on the back. Cornelius flailed in fear and itchy discomfort, but due to his small size and light weight, the snapworm easily dragged Cornelius back into the hole from which it had emerged, never to be seen again.

"No," said Kane. "He didn't deserve that. Confound this treacherous breed. I'm half-tempted to burn the whole nest of them when I arrive in person."

"Behind you!" Travis called.

Loudmouth turned to see that his two former captors, those merciless bickering snapworms, had finished fighting and were now extending themselves further, reaching like tentacles trying to grab him and drag him backward. Kane propelled Loudmouth forward and hopped across the finish line, securing his victory and tackling the delicious flower bud at the end.

"He did it," Travis shouted. "We won!"

The other orphans hooted with surprise and applauded, aside

from those who'd lost big in the betting phase and now watched their prized possessions snatched away by their rivals. They wept and grumbled.

Furter slapped Travis on the back and nodded to him, then extended a hand to signify that he had won fair and square. Travis accepted the gesture and shook Furter's hand, while noticing that Crump and Gulken lacked the same sportsmanship. They were both staring daggers at him now, ruing the moment they'd allowed the lucky birthday boy to race. Travis gave a conciliatory nod to Crump and Gulken, and scooped Loudmouth into his hands. Loudmouth was still munching away at the flower bud while Kane's voice moaned with delight.

"Oh, the flavors!" Kane spoke through mouthfuls. "This bug's palate is divine! A shame about Cornelius though. Such a cruel race it was."

Travis found it difficult to take Kane's condolences seriously since he was chewing and grunting all the while, but he decided not to judge the Vec too harshly. After all, Kane had piloted the little Loudmouth to victory. This was a time of celebration! *It had all been worthwhile,* thought Travis. *The hardship, the suffering. It all led me here! To my chance at escape!*

But before he could collect his coin, Gulken screamed as though he'd lost an arm.

GULKEN'S REVENGE

"Vonkenschtook," Gulken called. "Vonken-schtoooook!"

"What are you doing?" Crump asked, slapping Gulken across the gut.

"He cheated," Gulken said. "He killed my bug. He did it on purpose. He's a freak and a cheat! Vonkenschtook!"

"You'll get us all in trouble," said Furter, actively trying to cover Gulken's mouth.

"He doesn't deserve that coin," said Gulken, shoving the others away. "Vonkenschtook! They've stolen from you! Thief! Thief!"

No, thought Travis. The sounds of Vonkenschtook thundering upstairs were already audible. *It can't end like this*. Gulken was so vindictive that he didn't even care about getting the others in trouble. *How can he be so selfish?*

Vonkenschtook boomed into the room, practically ripping the door from its hinges. The children had no time to clean up the track, the evidence of gambling, or Vonkenschtook's unflattering caricature. They were caught in the act. Gulken had gotten his way. Now they were all doomed.

"What's this?!" Vonkenschtook screeched at the frozen orphans.

“What is the meaning of this debauchery? I finally unload one of you little rats and the rest of you go insane with hedonism? I should have tied you to the back of that carriage and had the Tree Man drag you in the streets!”

"It was Travis," said Gulken. "He stole your gold coin, and made us compete for it. He *made* us. He’s no good! It’s like you said!"

Gulken had somehow conjured up fake tears in a matter of moments. His eyes looked twice the size they were usually, brown pools of sorrow. It had been *Travis*! That dirty ne'er-do-well had led the boys astray.

Travis turned to Furter and Crump for support. *You must tell the truth,* thought Travis. *You’re the only ones who can save me. He’ll believe you!* He pleaded with his eyes. Furter and Crump were both silent, averting their gaze, staring at their toenails instead. *They don’t want to admit they stole the coin*, Travis realized.

Travis’s heart began pumping rapidly. His gut contracted, making it feel as though he might vomit. Everyone around him felt distant and hazy. The only truth in the universe was the imminence of Travis’s punishment.

“Look,” Gulken said, procuring the coin from Crump’s sleepsack. Gulken held it aloft for Vonkenschtook to see. “Travis stole it from you. He made us race the bugs. None of us wanted to do it. He made us.”

Travis felt like he was moving more slowly than the rest of them. When he turned his head, he could see some of the orphans nodding, verifying Gulken’s falsehood. They were willing to sell him out so long as they could protect themselves.

Vonkenschtook stepped forward, plucking the coin from Gulken’s fingers. He stared at the coin, eyed it for corruption, as he spoke to Travis.

"I should have known when you arrived under cover of night," said Vonkenschtook, in a tone so soft and direct that it might have been another man's voice, "when you were cradled in some outlaw's arms, begging for sanctuary, when I saw you writhing like a wretch, covered in burns and blood, that you would bring nothing but shame to this orphanage."

Vonkenschtook turned to Travis. The old man was smiling.

"I knew you were a mishap in the making," he said. "And though it pains me greatly to do this, I believe a short stint in the basement may cure you."

There were gasps from the others. They knew one boy had almost died down there. There was no food in the basement. The longest anyone had lasted before becoming a shambling, screaming wreck was three days.

"How-?" asked Travis, too frightened to resist further. "How long?"

"Three weeks," said Vonkenschtook. "If it does not cure you, the darkness may cure this house of your wickedness, one way or the other."

Vonkenschtook's arm shot forward, grabbed Travis by the hair and dragged him backward out the door. Travis screamed and protested, clutching Kane's bug in his fist, trying not to squish him while he screeched in pain.

"Your whining will not save you," said Vonkenschtook, pulling Travis down the stairs, bashing his backside on every wooden step, down into the kitchen, then through the living area, and towards the cellar door.

He swung the door open, and threw Travis down the basement stairs. It was worse than any beating from the boys. It felt like being beaten with logs, punched in the shoulder, then the hip, then against the side of the head, and finally the cold stone floor, where he skidded across, tearing his flesh, and groaning.

He could not see a thing but dancing stars. The pain had robbed him of coherence, but he could hear the slow methodical creaking of Vonkenschtook descending the stairs to watch him twitching in discomfort.

"Travis," Kane cooed from his palm. "Travis, my boy, speak to me! That villain! How could he do such a thing?! Travis, you must awaken! I cannot lose you now! Not like I lost your parents. Not after just meeting you. No! Travis!"

“What’s that clicking sound?” Vonkenschtook purred. “Your teeth?”

Travis trembled and lifted his head, blinking, bringing the orphan keeper into focus. He was a dark shadow outlined by the white light of the upstairs doorway. He seemed to be balling his fists, preparing for a further beating, but as Travis blinked away the stars he realized it was the tightened posture he rarely exhibited, the kind that meant Vonkenschtook was trying to restrain a laugh. He was not concerned for Travis’s well-being. He was joyous.

"I hear something,” said Vonkenschtook.

Travis was too weak from the fall to reach out and stop Kane from acting. The clever bug, the little Loudmouth, escaped Travis’s fingers and hopped toward Vonkenschtook, looking as though he was preparing to conjure a miraculous spell.

"Now see here, you sadist," said Kane. "I will not stand idly by while you torture this child. I shall defeat you with all the powers gifted to me! Prepare thyself!"

Vonkenschtook heard the clicking. He saw in the dim light the insect thrashing this way and that, its legs swirling like the branches of a willow in the wind, and with a single, clean motion, Vonkenschtook stamped the bug to death.

PUNISHMENT

"Loudmouth," Travis murmured, barely able to keep his eyelids open from the weight of the pain.

"Do not insult me further, you worm," said Vonkenschtook, scraping his boot on the ground to get the last remnants of the bug out from under it.

"You killed him," said Travis. "You ruined everything."

"Do not raise your voice to me again," said Vonkenschtook. "Or I will make sure there's nothing left of you. Let your time in the dark be a reminder to stay silent."

Travis winced and shut his eyes again, curling into a ball to keep himself from screaming. Tears ran down his cheeks to his lips so he could taste them.

Satisfied by the silence, Vonkenschtook went up the stairs and shut the door, locking it. That was the last hint of daylight Travis saw for some time.

Time lost all meaning in the darkness. Once he felt well enough to move slightly, he found a mossy patch growing in the place where the floor met the wall. He was able to lap up some water from it which had trickled in and pooled from outside.

The basement of the orphanage stored suits of armor from when the orphanage had been barracks for knights hundreds of years prior. Those suits of armor frightened the children, standing half-formed like skeletons, silently watching those who would descend the stairs. Now they were Travis's only companions, and like them, he found himself slowly rotting in the basement, unlikely to be rescued.

Eventually he pulled himself upright, using the busted metal suits for support. *Someday maybe I could be a knight,* thought Travis, but the unlikeliness of that dream made him chuckle. What point was there in hope when every opportunity would be filtered through Vonkenschtook's cruelty? He was too battered and broken to fight now. *There is no reason to argue,* he thought. *To talk back or mock him.* It would only result in more punishment, and if that punishment might lead him to this halfway point between life and death, he'd be better off not risking it.

A few days of starvation led Travis to eat dirt clods and straw. He used his fingers to scratch them free from the floor and shoved them into his mouth greedily.

The memory of the clever bug, Kane, the Vec or whatever he was, felt like a distant dream. It had been a fleeting moment of wonder, perhaps the result of trauma or delusion. There was no magic burbling within him like a witch's cauldron. Had he any innate ability, he would surely use it to free himself from this nightmare. *No,* he thought. *I heard the voice in my head because I am insane.*

At some point he heard what distinctly sounded like a ricktick crawling its way down the stairs.

"Piltik's feet," the bug said. "Could no one light a candle in this pit?"

Travis thought his imagination was playing tricks on him. *Yes,* he thought. *My brain is inventing a friend to save me.* How pathetic he felt to be pitied by his own mind. But he could not argue against his pitiable nature, and so he lay motionless, wallowing, accepting his fate as the recipient of wild hallucinations.

"Travis," the bug called. "Oh, Travis. Do be alright."

"Yes," Travis said, blandly. "I am doing just fine, thank you. The suits of armor and I have started a band of minstrels called The Basement Boys. Would you like to hear a verse of our latest ditty? It is titled, *Woe is We.*"

The bug seemed a bit startled by Travis' maudlin tone, pausing to collect itself before asserting, "I know you must have suffered greatly down here, and I am sorry. But we must escape together now to prevent further villainy."

Travis tilted upright, and could feel his hair falling over his eyes in the darkness. He forced his weight on his palms and sneered at the bug.

"Unless you've got a cannon inside your shell, you aren't doing much to help, now are you?" he asked.

"Well at least this punishment hasn't undermined your sense of humor," said Kane, scuttling closer. He had a little playfulness in his voice, hoping this jab might shake Travis out of his melancholy.

Travis could hear the bug in the darkness, but it was still impossible to see him clearly. It was all nonsense of course. Even if the bug was truly there, there was no way that some Vec named Kane actually wanted to save him.

"I'm trying my hardest to get there in person now," the bug said. "I should be there in a few days' time. Do you think you can hold on?"

Travis was sick of being promised the moon only to wind up in the gutter.

"Who says I want your help?" asked Travis. "If it weren't for you, I wouldn't be locked in the basement. Vonkenschtook is right to punish me. All I do is complain. Unlike you, he's given me a place to live, and food sometimes, of sorts. And..."

Travis could not successfully think of a third thing Vonkenschtook had given him.

"This sounds like a tale of the Fate of madness," the bug murmured. "You sound nothing like the boy I met a week ago. You need to find courage for the journey ahead. You must believe in your worth!"

"I'm not going anywhere with you," Travis said.

"Travis," said Kane. "Whether you like it or not, I'll be coming to save you. I suggest you resolve yourself to that fact before we have a most unpleasant journey together. If there is anything I can provide for you in the meanwhile, please let me know. But I will not tolerate your foul attitude, because I'm the only one in this bloody world who is trying to protect you."

Travis thought he knew where the little Loudmouth was now. He leaned forward, hoping the bug would sense this attempt at confidentiality.

"There is one thing you can get me," said Travis, lightening his tone a bit.

"Yes, my boy," said Kane, softening the edges of his voice. "What is it?"

With a lightning quick grab, Travis snatched the insect off the ground and shoved it into his mouth, chewing ferociously.

With a mouth full of ricktick, Travis continued.

"A proper meal," he said.

When Vonkenschtook finally decided to release Travis from the basement two weeks later, Travis showed little in the way of animosity toward the orphan keeper or the other boys who had betrayed him. In fact, he showed little emotion of any kind. He was now a dour muted specter of the boy he once was. He was pale and sallow-cheeked and wandered place to place like a bit of fabric in a breeze. He participated in Vonkenschtook's military drills, but he neither excelled or floundered. He merely existed, hoping his silence would buy him anonymity.

The other children ignored him, even Furter and Crump, likely because they were so ashamed of the role they'd played in his punishment. Gulken seemed to show mercy, not picking a fight or threatening him, but he didn't seem fully satisfied either, as if he still resented Travis in spite of everything. The days floated by, one into another, an endless stream of green and grey.

Two weeks of dullness passed and then suddenly, like a rap on the door in the middle of the night, something strange happened. A horse, rider-less and quite stubborn, came clopping up to the gates of Mercy Square. It was a jet black mare, beautiful with a flowing mane and the vibrance of springtime in its eyes. The guards tried shooing it away, but the horse kept scratching its hoof against the gate until the guards finally decided to let it inside and inspect it further. When the guards approached and tried to corral the beast, it reared up on its hind legs and neighed with disapproval. It then retreated toward the gathering crowd of townspeople, where it proceeded to dance and do delightful tricks for them. At this point the guards were too bewildered to do much but watch, and as the horse posed no immediate threat, they decided to shrug their shoulders and enjoy the chicanery with the rest of the town for however long it lasted.

Unable to keep the orphans from clamoring outside to join in the adoration of the horse, Vonkenschtook eventually agreed that they should all inspect the beast for hints of foul play. Travis was rightfully suspicious of the horse, for when he approached it, the horse turned its head and narrowed its eyes directly at him.

With a snort and a playful stomp of her hoof, the horse began inspecting Travis from head to toe, sniffing at him and biting his tunic, until it tasted something particularly foul caked into them, and released him, shaking its head.

The other children chuckled as the horse recoiled, joking to one another that even the horse could tell that Travis stank like pig slop. But before the horse lost all interest in Travis, its eyes rolled upward and became cloudy. Travis turned this way and that. The other people of the town were still chuckling at the horse as if they had no knowledge of this strange transformation. Then, when its eyes had mutated in form to something strangely human and familiar, Travis distinctly heard Kane's voice emanating from the horse's mouth.

"I shall be here shortly," said Kane's voice. "This time I've arrived in a form you couldn't possibly devour, unless you really *are* a savage child."

And with a sneeze that blasted snot directly onto Travis's face, the horse blinked its eyes and returned to its display of playful innocence, leaving Travis disgusted and goo-covered, while the others howled with laughter.

Travis tried to wipe what he could of the horse phlegm onto the front of his tunic, but found that it was so filthy that it would only make his face dirtier. He backed away from the crowd, they being too distracted by the horse to notice, and found a puddle of rainwater next to a pile of straw. He cupped his palms and splashed some of the water upon his face, trying to dry it and wipe it clean with the bristling end of the straw. As he did so, his heartbeat quickened with thoughts of vectory.

Kane is coming, he thought. Was the sneeze all the punishment the Vec had planned, or would there be worse things waiting for him? *Why did I eat that bug?* he thought. It was truly an act of savagery, as Kane the horse had suggested. *I wasn't even thinking clearly*. But he knew deep down that the source of his violent anger had been self-loathing, pity, and disgust. In an odd way Travis felt that he had earned the humiliation, that perhaps Vonkenschtook had been right all along, and that there was no one less worthy of rescue than he.

As the horse continued to delight the crowd, another visitor was spotted trotting his way down the path to Mercy Square. The guards could hear him babbling even from a distance, complaining of his ill-fitting boots and the mud that was ripping them off with every step. He looked to be an adult, halfway through the standard lifespan. He had long black hair, spectacles and a bent brown hat. He also had very long sleeves, the kind that a trickster might use for hiding things. He mucked his way to the Mercy Square gates, cursing at his feet all the while.

"Confound this wretched path," he said.

"Halt," said Mesto, the gate guardsman, a stern, plump fellow. "Who goes there?"

"A mud-sodden malcontent, as you can clearly see," said the traveler. "I don't mean to sound immediately ungrateful for your presumed hospitality, but I cannot believe whoever concocted this town thought it was a good idea to make it so inaccessible. Though I suppose to a certain extent, that would be the point."

"The point of what?" asked Mesto, genuinely mystified.

The traveler sighed loudly and dramatically.

"Yes, perhaps I'm getting wildly ahead of myself, likely to overcompensate for how long it's taken me to slog my way here without my horse."

"Your horse?" Mesto asked, glancing over his shoulder toward the black mare within the city walls. It seemed to be waiting for the gates to open expectantly.

"Aye," said the other guard, a bumbling sort by the name of Fleetfoot. "We've got a horse in here now that just came wandering up."

"Well of course you do," said the traveler. "This is the only village for miles, and she came trotting off in this direction, now didn't she? Why else would I be wading through this muck? She was rather cross with me that I'd run out of gupperfruit, a personal favorite of hers for whatever reason, and in her temperamental fury she betrayed my trust, and left me for dead."

Fleetfoot eyed the man suspiciously.

"You mean this is your horse then?" Fleetfoot asked.

The traveler groaned with exasperation.

"Yes, of course," he said. "That's precisely what I mean. Would you be so kind as to let me inside your gates so I might reacquire her?"

Fleetfoot stared at the man outside the gates, with his big floppy hat and long sleeves and thought this might be some sort of ploy to siege the town.

"Hold on," said Fleetfoot. "If this is your horse, if we even have a horse in here, then why aren't you the one that's riding her?"

The traveler shouted with frustration, sounding a bit like a child as he stomped his boot into the mud with great emphasis.

"Have I not just explained this much to you?" the man asked.

Fleetfoot took a moment to consider this, then slowly and resolutely said no.

Just as the traveler's face became red with rage and it was clear that the guards were about to receive a profanity-ridden tirade from the man, Mesto reined control of the conversation back from his cohort.

"Whoa there, floppy man," Mesto said. "What he means to say is, how much is that there horse worth to you?"

"Are you insinuating," the traveler sputtered, "that you wish to charge me a finder's fee for my own horse? A horse that was out of my company for less than a half hour? I'll have you know that your buffoonery will not only anger me, good sir, but it will anger the royal family! For if word gets back to the Clockwork Palace about this, you'll both be beheaded posthaste."

Mesto's eyes widened as though the man's speech had stunned

him. He turned to Fleetfoot, looking for some sort of solution. Fleetfoot scratched his chin and asked a simple yet poignant question.

"What?"

After another brief bit of shouting, the traveler explained who he was in detail.

"That horse, my darling Betsy, was a gift from Princess Gillifred! I was one of her tutors, and am still a dear friend of the royal family. As you can see from this seal on my robes, I am not some peasant for your beratement and amusement. I am Chief Royal Historian, Kane Verdalea! Who in the Fates' domain are you?!"

KANE VERDALEA

After the traveler forced some apologies from the guards, they opened the gates and allowed this Kane Verdalea into Mercy Square. The traveler sauntered about, his nose held high as if he were not covered in mud, and inspected the townspeople with one eyebrow raised, trying as best he might to seem dismissive.

"There she is," he said, his voice exhibiting a warble of relief upon locking eyes with his horse, his dearest Betsy.

Betsy, the black mare, clopped her hoof against the ground and nodded her head, snorting a bit as if challenging Kane to a race. He bowed to her coyly, then began circling her, dancing alongside her in a courtly manner. The townsfolk backed away and cleared a hole in the center of the congregation to watch as Kane and Betsy performed a practiced dance of intricate twirls and sidesteps. Based solely on the precision of the dance there could be no doubt that this man was the horse's rightful owner, if not its dance instructor.

Kane and Betsy bowed to the crowd and received a round of applause.

"Yes, well," Kane said. "There is no shame in showing ones pride in a happy reunion, even with a beast so contemptible."

Betsy whinnied with offense and shook her head in the negative.

"Well you did leave me to die in the woods just now," Kane complained.

Some of the townspeople had taken a liking to this odd pair, both so willful and eccentric. Travis remained unconvinced of Kane's altruism. He watched the scene unfold while squatting behind a haystack.

He truly is a strange man, Travis thought, eyeing Kane up and down.

"He's a traveling jester, is he?" asked Fleetfoot.

Kane did not let this minor transgression slide.

"No," Kane said, approaching Fleetfoot with wide-eyed focus. "Chief Royal Historian. I've just told you not five minutes past. Have you no mental retention? You've seen the seal. I can provide further documentation if required. I am a man of dignity, not some common buffoon."

To undermine Kane's point quite eloquently, Betsy bit him by the rump of his robes and pulled him backward, causing him to sway comically. The townspeople laughed at this, assuming it was another of the pair's trademark bits. The look on Kane's face said otherwise, and he shot the beast a particularly contemptible stare before steadying himself and trying to climb atop his dignity once more.

"Say," asked Mesto, the other guardsman, "why is it you was out this ways before you lost your horse?"

Mesto had a glimmer of something resembling intellect in his eye. Kane's confidence shrank a bit, but sprang back up joyously. Kane danced about his horse and retrieved a small scroll stowed in a saddlebag on Betsy's back. Kane procured it and unfurled it.

"As Royal Historian to the Queen of Krankfert, I, Kane Verdalea, do declare formally that I am allowed a small stipend, proclaim-able by means of this document, which stipulates as often one does when stipend-ing for the hire of a *research assistant.*" Kane cleared his throat while quickly closing the scroll. "And as I am the ripe old age of thirty-five-ish, and getting no younger I might add, I shall require a servant of reasonable strength and character."

Before Kane could explain himself further, Vonkenschtook shot forward to the front of the crowd like a jackrabbit spotting its mate.

"I run the orphan trade here, sir," said Vonkenschtook. "I am pleased to meet a fellow man of finery." With a conspiratorial round-the-collar grasp Vonkenschtook wrapped his fingers around Kane's neck and pulled Kane in close. "Don't trust the rest of these lot," the orphan keeper spat, his breath hot and scratchy. "They are low and unworthy."

Vonkenschtook released Kane and nodded twice in succession. Kane's lip curled. He could still smell Vonkenschtook's stench, even though the man had stepped backward. It was the curdled smell of death. Kane eyed the man vilely.

"And what would you know about class?" Kane asked him.

"I am Vonkenschtook," he cried. The townspeople grimaced, their eyes rolling from fatigue. "I run this whole bloody town. I'm sixty-third in line for the throne. What sort of historian are you if you haven't heard of me?"

"Of course I've heard of you," Kane replied. "Yes, the Queen told me to come inspect you. Should sixty-two other royals suddenly pass and you become the Queen, we want to make sure all of our hogs are in the right pen. Understand?"

Vonkenschtook's posture became rigid. Kane searched the crowd for Travis but could not see him. He closed his eyes like he was sniffing out an outhouse. He wandered forward then sprang upon Travis suddenly, leaping betwixt several villagers, startling them, and yanking Travis up from behind the haystack.

"Look at this lad," Kane suggested. "This is the work of your orphan keeper."

The townspeople shied away from the sight of Travis, the badly beaten, pale and skeletal boy.

"You don't want that one," Vonkenschtook shouted. "That one is a nightmare."

"Is that so?" asked Kane, releasing Travis's arm and stepping forward to confront Vonkenschtook. "Is he the kind of foul creature that might lock a child in the basement for weeks on end or beat the children he was sworn to protect?"

Vonkenschtook licked his lips. "I'll bet he is, bleeding demon of a boy! I wouldn't trust him. No, you'd prefer this one over here."

Vonkenschtook went over to Gulken and pulled him forward. Gulken tried to smile prettily to Kane. Kane was not impressed by this display of sycophancy, and waved him away. He gestured just toward Travis and said, "Let me just have this one for whatever pittance he's worth, and I'll be on my way."

"Well the costs," said Vonkenschtook, "are always considerable."

"Costs?" Kane asked. "Well, I'd agree. I did provide a fine horse show for you. Based on the quality of the dance and the disrespectful nature of the orphan in question, I should think that you'd be willing to part with him for free."

"That's bold-faced thievery," said Vonkenschtook.

Kane roared.

"And it is bold-faced abuse to treat these children in such a cruel and reprehensible manner," he said. "Are the other townsfolk aware that you threw young Travis in the basement and left him for dead? That you starve and scream at these children, destroy their possessions, and behave as a petty tyrant?"

"Now see here," said Vonkenschtook. "I do exactly as I must to keep these wretches in line. They're my property. And I deny these claims against me. I have been a loving orphan keeper, haven't I?"

The other orphans mumbled an indifferent sound in unison.

"Your actions speak for themselves," said Kane. "Guardsman, have ye a jail cell or a pillory in these walls?"

Fleetfoot responded. Pillory was a word he recognized.

"Aye, my lord. We have a stocks."

"Put this one inside until he agrees to treat his charges with more care," Kane said.

The guards exchanged a look of befuddlement. Fleetfoot shrugged and grabbed Vonkenschtook by the shoulders.

“He’s got a point,” he murmured.

Fleetfoot had grown up under Vonkenschtook’s care and had no love for the man. The feeling was apparently mutual, because Vonkenschtook elbowed Fleetfoot in the jaw to evade him. The guardsman’s head twisted sideways like he might spit a tooth. His jaw hung agape afterward, aghast that he had been struck so suddenly.

“Now see here,” cried Vonkenschtook. “I’m in line for the royal family and regardless of your political position I am blood of the family, and that makes you scum in comparison. I would need a trial before anyone could penalize me.”

“He struck me in the face,” said Fleetfoot. “Hang him!”

The crowd roared in unison, suddenly incensed by their common hatred for Vonkenschtook. Their animosity toward the man surprised even Kane.

“I am acting on the Queen’s behest and the Princess’s behalf and the beekeeper’s beehives, so plop on your thirty-thousandth in line for all I care. My royal summons outranks whatever flimsy claim you purport to own,” spake Kane.

“Friends,” said Vonkenschtook, appealing to the crowd. “Is it not strange for an outsider to come by this information? Is it not strange his sudden appearance, just after the Tree Man that arrived last month? Do not these men share common suspiciousness?” Vonkenschtook gestured to Kane’s flowing robe.

The crowd eyed Kane’s garb. It wasn’t flashy, but he did have that odd tinge about him like he might have some connection to vectory. Kane caught scent of this turning of the tides. Vonkenschtook had pivoted the crowd’s attitude into suspicion toward

Vecs, those magic-using outlaws who were the root of all the world's ills, according to a large swath of Krankferters.

"What's this?" Kane chuckled. "A *Tree Man*? You are delusional."

Fleetfoot took no pause in grabbing Vonkenschtook again, firmly this time.

"Wait," Vonkenschtook cried. "How could he know about the basement? There was no one there but myself and the boy! And he called him by name! Travis, he called him. But I've never seen this man before in my life. How would he know about so lowly a boy? He must have used vectory! He's a Vec!"

No one was laughing at Kane now. They were eying him silently, wondering if he might summon some awful spell at any moment. The orphans who had been previously enthralled with Betsy were now backing away from her. A few of the children threw dirt clods at her, causing her to kick backwards and knock an elderly woman over onto her hip. The crowd shouted in the negative.

Kane began to sarcastically swagger. He wandered over to a nearby bush and reached deep inside of it. "Oh, yes," Kane said, mocking Vonkenschtook. "I'm a real Vec, aren't I? Look, I can make a rabbit appear from this bush. Hmm. Now hang on, there actually is something in here..."

Kane found a copy of *Wonky's Krankferten Monsters* from where Travis had thrown it earlier. Some members of the crowd gasped to see such magic. Kane *tsk*-ed and rolled his eyes at them, still trying to dismiss the accusation.

"That's *my* book," said Vonkenschtook. "He's stolen it."

"That does it," shouted Kane.

The crowd stopped their mob tactics and fell silent. Kane turned to them, smiling villainously. He began to cackle.

"You've found me out, have you?" Kane said. "You think the Queen, noted hater of Vecs, would let a Vec in her own employ? You think my robes unfashionable? You think my documentation forged? Have you ever seen such finery?"

The crowd was not convinced.

"Oh, very well then," said Kane.

He extended his arm and a small metal rod shot forth. He caught it neatly in his hand and flipped a latch on its side, which caused the rod to triple in length. The crowd gasped to see this feat of mechanical engineering.

"Impressed, are you?" asked Kane. "This is no magic. This is a gift from the Princess. However I can do one little trick with it. Would you like to see?"

With a *POOF*, a cloud of smoke puffed out of the end of Kane's rod. A few yards away, as Fleetfoot was wrestling with him, Vonkenschtook disappeared. And in an instant, a few feet lower and flapping manically, there was a chicken.

The crowd marveled at the transformation. Vonkenschtook was now a chicken.

"Vec!" screamed a man, and soon they were all squawking like chickens too, begging for help and stepping over one another to escape from Kane.

Kane grabbed Travis, set him upon Betsy, and climbed atop her himself. Addressing the orphans, Kane gestured toward the Vonken-chicken.

“You all look famished,” he said. “Might I suggest a meal?”

Some of the more vengeful orphans were already trying to strangle the chicken. Off it went, screeching back into the orphanage. They chased after it, causing a bit of an uproar in the process. The townspeople internally debated whether to fear the Vec or chase after the free meal, and if they did the latter, would that mean potentially devouring the orphan keeper? While they tried to decide, Kane tipped his hat and carried Travis off into the forest of No Mercy.

THE WORLD BEYOND

Low-hanging branches, twisted wooden limbs, gnarled roots and shaking leaves sailed behind Travis and Kane as Betsy the black mare carried them deeper into the forest of No Mercy. They had only been gone a few moments, and Travis was already deeper into the forest than he had ever been in his entire life.

The path was narrow and muddy, much of it overgrown, but Betsy raced along it, easily evading the fallen logs and bramble patches.

"Where are we going?" asked Travis.

"Someplace safe," Kane answered.

"Safe for who?" Travis wondered.

Kane paused to consider this reply.

"Safe for both of us," said Kane.

Travis clung to Kane's belly as they rode swiftly down the path.

"I've never been on a horse before," said Travis.

Travis thought that he might vomit.

"Slow down, Loudmouth," Travis said.

With a bit of a shudder Kane pulled at the horse's reins.

"Please don't call me that absurd name any longer," said Kane. "It's absolutely unbearable. Instead call me Kane, or sir, or something respectable."

"You're not really a historian," said Travis. "Are you?"

"Now listen here, Travis," Kane said. "There are many things you do not understand about this world. Some of them may come as quite a shock."

"You said you knew my parents," Travis said. "But they're dead. They've been dead since I was young."

"I knew them before they were dead," said Kane. "Before you were born. Back when they lived at The Palace."

"The Palace," Travis murmured. "The Clockwork Palace?"
"Travis," Kane said. "You'll have to keep much of what I tell you to yourself. I can't have you blurting out your origins to every passing moth or stray woodland creature. The forest has eyes and ears, the same as a man does."

Travis remembered the Tree Man and thought this might be true. Even so, Kane's knowledge of Travis's past was far too tantalizing to ignore.

"You must tell me everything now," said Travis. "Or I will tell one of the local patrols that you kidnapped me."

"Travis," Kane said, losing his patience. "We are pursued, even now by our enemies, those who wish to spill our blood. Can we please retire to a safer location before bellowing our darkest secrets?"

Kane's point was clear. They rode for a while in silence, until it became so dark that Betsy nearly took a tumble on a cluster of roots. Kane, cursing, decided they'd traveled far enough and stopped at the least brambly part of the roadside.

When Kane swung himself off the horse the world seemed to ripple around him, as if his impact had shaken the fabric of reality. He spoke in a strange foreign tongue and his words appeared to bend the branches of the trees. From out of his left sleeve his rod shot forth. He grabbed it deftly. With a flick of his wrist the rod tripled in length. Now it was a full staff, brimming with a white orb of light at the end. Kane began to wave it wondrously, bending the ethereal light where the pollen met the trees.

"Now Travis," Kane said, turning to the lad with a conspiratorial gaze. "What I am about to show you would be considered highly illegal, and therefore must be kept a secret, for both our sakes. You've seen how the commoners don't trust our kind."

Closing his eyes and humming strangely, as if resonating with the forest itself, its noises and chirps, the rubbing of cricket legs, the croaking of frogs, the clicking of rickticks, Kane gently lifted the staff above his head and kissed it against some overhanging branches. As the branches met the staff, they began to radiate with a golden glow that illuminated the area overhead, spreading slowly like water bathing the shore. Soon a cluster of illuminated leaves were glowing overhead, giving Kane a lantern-like field of vision with which to conduct his work.

Travis tried to keep mum, biting his lip to prevent words from escaping him, but eventually the sight of the glowing leaves was so beautiful that he could not help but breathe loudly and rapidly, tilting upward at the wondrous magic.

With a swish of his staff and a tumult of wind, a minor tornado spun from the extension of Kane's arm and struck the trees around him. Shuddering and creaking, as if in pain from the gesture, the trees began to split and bend, bowing worshipfully to Kane. Branches shaved themselves off the sides of the trees. Leaves exploded off the limbs and fluttered to the ground. The treetops cracked off and either fell to earth or were caught by the limbs of their still standing comrades. Now there were fewer trees, but logs a plenty, rolling and bouncing forth.

Travis could feel the wind of the small tornado rustling his hair and ragged clothing, but he dared not take his eyes off the spectacle before him to adjust his appearance. All at once the broken trees, the logs and limbs and branches, danced as a family, shuffling and arranging themselves in a calculated manner. From the forest ground a structure emerged, constructed of the semi-sentient trees as they stacked themselves upon one another and formed what looked to be a perfectly hospitable cabin in a matter of seconds.

Before Travis realized that the spell had concluded, a home nicer than any he'd known in years appeared in front of him. Inexplicably there were already smoke rings puffing out from the top of a chimney, as though this place had always existed, and that the two travelers had simply happened upon it. Lantern lights within the cabin glowed brightly, and the door creaked open as if the whole cottage were beckoning them inside.

Kane stamped his staff upon the ground twice and it shortened on command, returning to its smaller, sleeve-friendly size, whereupon he stowed it, brushed a few loose leaves off his person and walked inside the cabin, closing the door carelessly behind him, as if Travis wasn't even invited. Travis sputtered and twitched and gasped and turned to Betsy as though she might have an explanation for what he'd just witnessed, but to the horse, such acts of vectory were perfectly normal. She snorted slightly, surprised that Travis was still waiting outside. Travis took the hint, rushed over and opened the door.

It was a blessing of Diadra, the Fate of good fortune. There were wooden rocking chairs by the fire, a small table filled with alchemical supplies, and a bookshelf piping with strange tomes. But most blessed and satisfying of all was the banquet upon the round center table, a whole roast turkey, cooked forest peas, sliced carrots, a bouquet of edible flowers, and an assortment of ale and cider.

Kane was already seated and eating from a plate piled high with food.

"Well don't just lurk in the doorway," Kane said. "Sit, eat. I imagine you're starving, and perhaps have been for some time. I hope this is to your liking."

"To my liking?" Travis asked. “It’s a miracle.”

Kane chuckled warmly. Travis crept toward the meal, certain that its beauteous arrangement must be evidence of a trap, that at any moment Vonkenschtook could pop out from one of the adjoining rooms and strike him fifty times on the head with his spoon. Kane was starting to look very impatient now.

"There's nothing to fear, you'll find," said Kane. "The spell I cast to produce this cabin should shield us from detection."

Kane realized then that this was more than a matter of food to Travis. He saw the boy frozen, his eyes glassy, muscles tensed.

"Travis," Kane said. "If your parents were here, do you know what they’d say?"

"What?" Travis asked.

"They would say, shut the door! Eat while it's hot!" He belched.

Travis was shocked by this. He shut the door and seated himself. Then at once, he was gorging, stuffing himself with grub to the point of choking, washing it all down with cider and moaning with delight at the joys of a full stomach while laying backward on the floor, happy for the first time in years. Kane was still seated at the table, watching Travis writhe on the ground.

"Yes," Kane said, "We'll have to work on your table manners at a later date. But I'm sure the Princess will be delighted to learn that you appreciated the feast."

"The Princess?!" Travis erupted, trying to sit up but being so full that this minor task felt impossible. He groaned and rolled to his side.

"Why yes of course," Kane said, as if this matter were perfectly ordinary. "Who do you think procured us such a feast? I won't have you thinking I eat like a duchess every evening. I merely kept the food preserved with a simple enchantment so that it would be fresh and ready the moment we settled for the evening."

"But what does the Princess have to do with me?" Travis asked.

"Ah," Kane said. "She's one of your few admirers. Well, more an admirer of myself and your mother, but you know, you're a fine proxy."

"My mother," Travis said.

"Yes," Kane replied. "The Princess models herself after your mother, you know. She has no magical aptitude of her own unfortunately. She obsesses over technical things, science, the low arts as it were. Still she seems cursed by the Fates to root for you. I think she sees you as a kindred spirit in a way."

Kane seemed lost in thought, pondering this last point in an oddly paternal manner.

"You look as though you might be sick," Kane noted. "Please do so outside."

Travis stood up, uncertain of what he might do.

"Now, now," Kane said. "There'll be plenty of time to discuss ancient history tomorrow. You need to rest. You'll be happy to find that this cabin has real beds, not just the sleep-sacks you poor orphans used."

Travis entered the room behind him to find a real bed with pillows and blankets.

Maybe I'll test it out, Travis thought. *Just to see how soft it is.*

And as soon as Travis's head hit the pillows he was adrift in the land of dreams.

GIFT OF THE PRINCESS

Travis woke suddenly to the sound of Kane chiding him for oversleeping.

"Come, Travis," said Kane, as if they were mid-conversation. "We mustn't dawdle."

"To meet the Princess," Travis said, half-awake.

Kane chuckled. "No, not to meet the Princess, though it is alarming to think you may have been dreaming about her. You haven't even met her yet."

"Uh," Travis blushed. "I wasn't."

He absolutely had been. He had dreamt that the Princess had kissed him, and he fell several stories immediately afterward, as if dropped from the window outside her tower. The first part of the dream had felt alright, but the second part had not. He was having trouble shaking the grogginess and discontent the dream had instilled within him. And under no circumstances did he wish to admit the kissing part of the dream to Kane.

"Well, you're in luck," Kane responded.

“She’s here?!” Travis screeched.

He clutched at his covers to hide himself. Kane guffawed riotously.

“Nay,” he said, and Betsy whinnied. “She left you a steed instead.”

Travis lowered his covers cautiously. *What could he mean by steed?*

Kane wandered into Travis’s room casually.

“Say,” Kane asked. “Why are you still filth-ridden? Shouldn’t you have tidied yourself up a bit? Here, I shall help you.”

With a snap of his fingers, Kane’s rod shot forth from his sleeve. He flicked a switch on its side and it extended. Kane swirled the rod around in the air and aimed it at Travis threateningly.

“With the strength of a thousand seas,” he bellowed.

Travis’s bed erupted, collapsing inward, revealing a large heated cauldron beneath the floorboards. Travis tumbled inside like a ricktick into a watery bucket.

“A trap,” Travis cried. “I knew it was all a trap!”

Kane chuckled menacingly.

“Yes, I’ve tricked you into cleaning yourself. What a vile man am I!”

Travis did not like Kane’s tone, but as he splashed and sputtered, he realized that the water was rather pleasant. He turned to

Kane with a confused look.

"I've not meant to boil you," he explained. "I've meant for you to clean your muddy exterior so you will no longer offend polite society."

"A bath," Travis declared. "So this is the way of the wealthy."

He submerged himself in the water as if taking part in a sacred ceremony.

"We'll never be out of here at this rate," Kane muttered.

Kane left him to bathe, telling him to check the cupboard in the corner of the room after he was finished. Later when Travis did so, he found a new tunic and boots. He donned them, tossing his old rags out the window.

Newly dapper, Travis exited the house sniffing at his clothing.

"They smell funny," he admitted. "Is that the Princess's perfume?"

"That is the smell," Kane explained, "of not being covered in one's own excrement, my dear boy."

"I'm not sure I like it," he replied.

Kane grimaced and gestured toward the large object at Betsy's rear. It was half Betsy's size but hidden beneath a brown cloth. Someone had tied a red ribbon around the cloth concealing this mysterious object, as if it were a prize.

"Is that my present from the Princess?" Travis exclaimed.

"Yes," Kane said. "She so wanted to meet you, but because of the task at hand we shan't visit her for some time."

"We're going to the Clockwork Palace?" Travis asked.

"Not so loud," Kane whispered. "Spies and all that."

"Right," Travis said, trying to muffle his excitement. "Can I open it?"

"Yes," Kane said. "But just to be clear... the Princess's tastes are quite eclectic."

"What do you mean?" asked Travis.

"She... designed it herself," Kane shrugged. "You'll see."

Travis could not contain himself any longer. He snatched at the ribbon, unraveling it in the air like a scarlet snake dancing in the trees. He tore at the cloth, biting it with his teeth to tear it open. Kane watched him perform this task with revulsion. Even Betsy seemed shocked. When he'd finished prying the thing open he revealed something he did not comprehend.

Before him, in the place where his gift should be, was a silver horse-like statue. It had been crafted out of metal, and while it did sort of resemble a horse, there was nothing particularly beautiful about it. It had large ovular eyeballs and an open mouth, as if it was braying. There was nothing intimidating or sleek about it. It almost looked like the construction of a mad-man.

Travis turned to Kane, suddenly suspicious. "Did the Princess really make *this*?"

Kane sighed. Travis could see it too. "Yes, it is beneath her isn't it?" He began pacing at Betsy's side. "She is a natural leader, and yet she dresses in common stylings and spends her days working on strange things like this. Mechanical oddities that have no purpose in the modern world."

Travis turned back to the horse-thing, whatever it was. "So she makes things."

"I told her that there is a chance her royal bloodlines have some vectory within them," Kane said. "But no, she resists. She wants to be like your mother, a great inventor. But the age of inventions died with Elaina."

This was the first Travis had heard his mother's name spoken aloud since he was a child. Images of his home, his hearth, the books on the shelves above the stove, and his father flashed in his mind.

"I'm sorry, Travis," said Kane. "I should not speak your mother's name. I'm sure the thought of your parents' demise fills you with complicated feelings. However, we must not mire ourselves in discontent. This is a happy occasion."

Travis found what appeared to be a rod jutting out of the horse-statue's spine. He tried to retrieve it, but found it would only loosen when pulled a specific way. When he managed to switch it from one position to another, the statue began glowing with electricity. It warbled with a buzzing sound. With a gust of steam emitting from its short legs, the statue fired to life, hovering a foot off the ground. Travis stepped backward hoping it would not explode with this newfound power.

"Don't be scared of it," said Kane. "It's just a machine of some kind."

"What is it?" asked Travis.

“It’s something the Princess calls... a Hover-Donk.”

“A Hover-Donk?!”

It was clear to Travis now. The Princess had made some sort of hovering donkey. It looked to be an attempt to mechanically re-invent a horse. Betsy stamped her hoof, clearly considering this pseudo-beast to be some sort of ill-mannered rival.

"Come, Travis," said Kane, climbing atop Betsy. "We haven't enough time to dawdle. We're headed South. See if you can ride that thing.”

Before Travis knew what was happening, Kane had ridden Betsy back down the path toward the main road. He could hear Betsy clopping off in the distance.

“Hey! Wait!” Travis called.

Travis wondered if it might be safer to just stay in the cabin, but when he turned back, the cabin had already vanished. The trees had replenished themselves soundlessly. There was no evidence that he'd even been there, aside from the Hover-Donk.

Suddenly panicking that Kane had deserted him, Travis climbed atop the Hover-Donk and grabbed what appeared to be the metal approximation of reins. When he shoved them, the Hover-Donk floated forward. Moaning a bit as he wobbled to-and-fro, Travis eventually got the hang of the Hover-Donk’s basic controls, learning enough to be able to pilot himself back-wards, forwards, and side-to-side with some careful tilting and shifting. Not wanting to let Kane and Betsy get too far ahead of him, Travis considered this basic lesson to be enough practice for now and flew around the corner after them, deeper into the forest.

It seemed that the harder Travis pushed the bar, the deeper it sunk into the back of the Hover-Donk, which in turn gave the Donk some extra thrust, powering some sort of flame at the Donk's rear. As Travis pushed the bar harder, he could feel himself gain speed. The green and yellow and brown began to blur around him, though he swore he saw some red swish by him on the right.

No, he gasped. *It cannot be.*

He had seen that color once before.

The jarters prey on the weak and defenseless, he thought.

He lost control of the Hover-Donk as his mind wandered. He nearly dented the thing against the massive gnarled root of an ancient tree. He slowed his speed and tried to regain his control of the Donk, but while slowing himself he'd gotten turned the wrong way, and now he was somehow facing backward while traveling forward. That was when the noises hit him. *Ook*-ing and chattering rustling from the branches nearby. *The jarters*, he thought. *They're here.*

From the leaves their tails shot upright, dancing in distraction. Then from the other side of the road, a pack of jarters swung in from the branches above, firing barbs from their tails and shouting their battle cry. They were blood red and menacing. The yellow fur around their mouths announced the bright white of their gleaming teeth. They were the reason the forest was called No Mercy.

Travis saw the barbs sailing through the trees and knew that he had to speed away from them, but he was still turned a bit off course and had no idea how to slow his rotation. In order to move correctly in the right direction, he would need to wait until the Donk slowly turned the right way before accelerating, but that meant spending more time with the jarter horde.

These packs of predators, specific to southern Krankfert, a practically ancient indigenous influx from the Grimalkin Entanglement, had eaten all the wild boar in the area. Anything with a pulse was food to jarters, and with Kane leaving Travis unprotected he might as well have been a turkey leg laying in the road.

It's probably best not to think about that, Travis told himself, as a barb whizzed by his ear. *Come on, come on, you stupid thing!*

He was seconds away from being able to accelerate the Hover-Donk without immediately smashing into another tree.

RAH-AH-AH! A jarter howled in his ear. He could feel its hot breath, and so he jammed the bar forward, slicing some bark off the closest tree and rocketing back down the path toward Kane.

He could hear their vengeful screams behind him, the sound of branches cracking under their violent pursuit. And then, like a star guiding a lost soul in the night, he saw Kane's silhouette on the trail ahead, Betsy trotting gently as if waiting for the boy to catch up. Travis would easily outpace them.

Travis flew past Kane, screaming, "Jarters! Run for your lives!" Kane was a bit perplexed. He'd been in deep thought about Travis's emotional state. He had not considered other threats. *Could this be little more than a prank?* He wondered.

That was when the jarters leapt upon him, three of them, one atop his back, biting at his hat and hair. Another bit at Betsy's rear, snapping at her rump like a guard dog at a roast ham. The third leapt atop Betsy's head and covered her eyes.

Kane screamed at the top of his lungs and lunged the horse sideways. Betsy followed his direction, plunging toward a thicket of brambles. Travis slowed the Hover-Donk and re-approached Kane, seeing that the jarters were still giving them both a taste of Dorian, the Fate of death. Kane was holding Betsy's reins with one hand, tearing a jarter off his face with the other.

Travis raced past Kane and Betsy in the other direction, spun around behind them, and grabbed the jarter at Betsy's rear. It snapped at him and bristled with spiky fur as Travis heaved it back into the bushes. A thunder storm formed around Kane's skull as he raged against the beasts. Flickers of electricity glinted like daggers in Kane's eyes. Thunder rumbled and sent the jarters scampering off into the brambles from whence they came. As the last glimpses of their red tails disappeared amidst the forest greens, the storm abated.

"What was that?" asked Travis, pulling his Hover-Donk up alongside Kane.

"But a small sampling of my power," Kane said.

There was a cacophony of jarter cries. There were dozens of them now, reinforcements swinging through the trees at a rapid pace.

"Ride," said Travis, waving his hand wildly.

“Follow me,” cried Kane as he rode Betsy ahead.

Travis followed, the jarter barbs striking the ground around him as he accelerated. The road twisted left along a river, curving so that Travis had to tilt the entirety of the Hover-Donk at an angle to turn it. This meant the toe of his right boot was constantly in danger of scraping the ground. He tried not to trip the Hover-Donk up and spin out, but he could barely concentrate on doing so as several of the jarters flanked him from the sides, swinging between branches and gained momentum as he tried to escape. One hooted villainously and fired a barb from its tail directly into Travis's shoulder. He shrieked as the spikes pierced his skin. Blood flew in the wind behind him as he piloted the Hover-Donk, now in pain from the piercing. The jarters hooted with delight.

With a massive thunder crash a lightning bolt struck a tree in front of Travis, severing it into a stump. The tree trunk and branches fell forward towards Travis. He narrowly evaded them, ducking and swerving as they sailed overhead. The new-born log collided with eight of the jarters and took them for a roll in the opposite direction. They moaned in pain and fury.

"Sorry," Kane called to Travis from up the road.

Travis breathed heavily as he tried to remain calm.

The remaining jarters chased them for a few miles, until they came to a fork in the road and the horde's roar receded. They rested for a moment, and Kane removed the spike from Travis's arm with a soothing healing spell. He sang a strange incantation, and the sounds of gentle chimes and chirping birds sailed by Travis. He could feel a warm summer breeze. The spike disintegrated, as if carried away by this new magical sensation. And then like that, the pain was gone. Travis's wound had healed. He stared at the place where the barb had been.

"You really can do anything," Travis said.

"I wish that were the case," Kane said. "If that were true I could simply bring the dead back to life and end all this silly non-sense."

Kane led them toward their next destination, a distant city in the outskirts of the kingdom, opposite the direction of Clockwork City. When Travis realized he was no longer headed toward the Clockwork Palace's spire, he started to complain.

"We're going the wrong way," said Travis.

"We aren't going to Clockwork City quite yet," Kane said, slowing Betsy down so he could talk to the boy without shouting. "We need to make a stop. Your parents left you something very important at Southerner's Roost. Or rather, something very important your parents left you was later stolen, then sold, and now resides at Southerner's Roost. In fact, it's a relative wonder the Queen hasn't seized it already. I think because of Ducat Duncan's family name, he considers his museum a part of the Queen's treasury, but I somehow doubt she'd see eye-to-eye with that. In any case, we're going to steal it for ourselves."

"Steal it?" said Travis. "The Princess wants us to steal a sword?"

"Forget the Princess for a second," said Kane. "This is bigger than she is."

"Bigger than the Princess?!" Travis exclaimed.

"Yes, Travis," said Kane. "There are some things beyond even Gillifred. Though I'm sure she'd agree with you that anything beyond her is simply waiting to be conquered through some textbook or schematic or other."

The book, Travis thought. Mention of some textbook or other had reminded Travis of his Book of Creatures, the one he'd pilfered from Vonkenschtook.

"The book," he wailed. "I left it behind."

"Book?" asked Kane. "Do you mean *Wonky's Krankferten Monsters*?"

Kane slowed the horse down a bit and reached into one of Betsy's saddlebags.

"If so, I have it right here," he held it aloft. Noticing the look of delight on Travis's face, he tossed the book with a bit of vectory, spinning it in the air so it landed gently in Travis's arms.

"Wow," Travis said. "You saved it! Thank you, Loudmouth."

This angered Kane, who did not enjoy the reminder.

"You don't still think of me as that little bug, do you? You chewed me to pieces," Kane exclaimed. "Do you have any idea how that feels?"

"I'm sorry," said Travis. "I was starving."

"Yes," Kane said uncomfortably. "Well, don't eat me ever again."

"I promise I won't," Travis swore.

They rode a bit longer down a pleasant and gently curving patch on the main road. It was less thorny and dangerous than the road to Mercy Square. Kane had been dodging his questions, but Travis wanted answers.

"What was that about a sword before?" Travis asked.

"Yes," Kane explained. "There is the small matter of *stealing* it."

"We have to steal the sword," Travis said.

"Well, not we in fact, but you," said Kane. "I won't be there."

"What?" Travis shouted. "Why won't you be there? I thought

you were adopting me. Not that I want to call you 'Dad' but, still, you know, protect me!"

"That was just a ruse," said Kane. "You are an orphan still. I will teach you as best I can but in order for this plan to work you must deliver your own miracles."

Travis did not believe he had any miracles to deliver.

"You've lost your mind," said Travis.

"You have a choice, Travis," said Kane. "Run away, live in fear, or find the secret of the sword that your parents made for you. What do you say?"

"I'm no thief," said Travis.

Travis suddenly felt a pang of guilt. *The book*, he thought. He was holding it with one hand and recalling how he'd stolen it from Vonkenschtook. *Not only that*, Travis realized. Kane had revealed that he was a Vec to all of Mercy Square. Travis was still traveling with an outlaw. There was a chance that word would not spread from Mercy Square, but if Vonkenschtook somehow survived or stopped being a chicken, it could be dangerous for Kane as well.

"No one *wants* to be a thief," said Kane. "That's just the problem with the world today! Everything's illegal. Our very lives are a sin. So why not throw caution to the wind and see where a life of crime can take us? Within reason of course."

Kane, sensing Travis's disgust, sighed and said, "Fine. Well, you'll find some way of reasoning with Ducat Duncan, a notoriously unreasonable man, and everything will work out swimmingly. Let's try to ride a bit faster, shall we?"

Kane rode Betsy further down the path, past a broken down carriage. Travis hollered after him, but Kane was speeding away from the chat.

Once Travis finally caught up to Kane he shouted, "If my parents made this sword for me why does someone else have it?"

Kane sighed dramatically. "Let's scream about the robbery at the top of our lungs, why don't we? Honestly, Travis, trying to plan a heist with you is exhausting."

Travis furrowed his brow. "I want a real answer."

Kane *tsk*-ed. He sighed again. "Ducat Duncan has the sword," he spoke quickly and discreetly. "He is a rather pompous man and a collector of fine things. To him the sword is nothing more than a jewel, but in that way it is a prized jewel, the centerpiece of his collection. You will need to infiltrate his museum of finery and procure the sword from its bindings. Once afterward we shall meet again."

"Why don't you do it?" asked Travis. "Are you chicken? Is that why you can turn people into one? Are you some sort of chicken wizard?"

"No!" Kane cried, a bit defensively. "I'm simply too old to join Ducat's society of knights. And I'm not physically gifted either. I apologize, but you'll have to carry this burden alone. Given your special abilities, you should be fine."

"What special abilities?" asked Travis.

"Oh, Travis," said Kane. "You must come to terms with your vectory. I know it is a hard discovery for every young person in this country who inherits it, to realize you are an outlaw by nature, but it does not mean you are wrong, or were born badly, or any such nonsense. It is just a silly rule, and in other places, they don't have it. If all goes well, we shall visit one of those places for an extended stay, but right now we must focus on the task at hand. Reuniting you with the sword."

"Tell me more about the sword," Travis said.

"It is a solid gold sword with several runic indentations. The runestones have been removed, as they are illegal due to their imbued vectory, and so Ducat Duncan has set three gemstones in the places where the runestones used to be. Which means we can take or leave those, depending on how morally flexible you become."

Travis considered this. Was it right to steal a jewel embedded in something made for you, even if the jewel itself was not yours?

"Oh, also, there's one other part of the plan," Kane stammered.

Before Travis could inquire about it, Kane clicked a button on his rod and several grappling hooks shot forth from the sides of the Hover-Donk, wrapping around Travis and tying him to the mechanical creature like a prisoner.

MINION OF THE MAENADS

Travis struggled to release himself from the ropes or slide off the Hover-Donk somehow, but the grappling hooks had shackled themselves so efficiently to the undercarriage of the Hover-Donk that Travis was trapped in place. He found himself in a bit of an awkward position. Travis was tied to the Hover-Donk backwards, facing its rear, placing his face in close proximity to the donkey's backside. Travis could barely budge, and the Hover-Donk was difficult to steer in this position. Kane lashed a rope to the Donk and held the end of it, guiding it behind him like a lost little lamb.

"Let me go," Travis said. "You didn't tell me this part of the plan!"

"To be honest, I'm still a little miffed that you ate me," Kane replied.

Kane hummed merrily over Travis's curse words and objections to this buffoonery. As they rode through the trees they came to a small rectangular clearing in which maenads and oblings were dancing. It seemed as though the maenads had claimed the left side of the clearing and the oblings were vying for the right. The oblings were small and red but not frightening like jarters. They were about the size of an adult human's fist, round with little horns. They wielded their own tails as pitchforks. They were poking at the dancing maenads. The maenads did not seem threatened, dancing between flower petals, scattering dew drops.

"What's all that?" asked Travis, perking his head up from the butt of the Donk.

"Pay no attention to them," Kane said. "They have so many squabbles. They wish only to distract us. Short life spans, very petty arguments. Not very intelligent."

Travis was distracted indeed. The maenads, small and green haired, danced beautifully, leaving shimmering trails of wispy vectory. Travis realized they were indeed magic creatures, meaning they too were technically outlaws.

"Kane," said Travis. "Are the maenads not outlaws?"

"What?" Kane asked. "No, they're not dangerous. They're naturally occurring, and they mainly keep to themselves. Although I wouldn't be surprised if the Queen were to declare war on them for being a distraction from her beauty."

Travis wondered why Kane had such a disrespectful view of the Queen. *Perhaps he really does know her as well as he claims,* he considered.

One of the little red oblings stabbed at a maenad with its tail, causing the maenad to cry out in pain. Travis could not stand to see such brutality.

"Leave them alone," Travis said.

The fighting between the little creatures stopped. They all rushed over to Travis and began babbling at once, trying to get him to settle their grievances.

“What did I say?” asked Kane in a beleaguered voice.
"Oh thank you," said one of the maenads.

Soon all of the maenads were buzzing around Travis's face, inspecting his ropes and laughing at the strange mechanical donkey.

"Donkey Butt, Donkey Butt," they called.

"Don't call me that," said Travis. "My name is Travis."

"Travis, Travis, Donkey Butt," they sang in unison. Somehow they all knew the words already. It was truly some vectory. Travis understood why Kane had not wanted to meddle in their affairs. Now the little round oblings were laughing at him, rolling around gleefully and trying to join in on the fun.

The large round leader of the oblings sang, "Human, human! Give us your coin, human. If you do, we’ll kill you, and take even more!”

“Do you see?” said Kane. “That’s not even a reasonable offer! It is better to let them go their merry way, content with their squabbles.”

The maenads began to pull Travis’s hair and pinch his cheeks.

"Please stop," Travis begged.

"Donkey Butt, Donkey Butt," they sang. "Give us a kiss, Donkey Butt."

"Do not kiss them," cried the oblings. "They are tricksters!”

"You vile creature," Kane said to Travis. "Do not go about kissing low creatures like a nymph of the forest. We are men on a mission."

Trying to win Travis's favor, one of the oblings stabbed a maenad. She screamed and dissipated into a shadow of herself, ethereal and blue. It slowly faded away. Her friends screamed and began bullying the obling that had slain her, shoving it and screaming vile statements at it. Kane told Betsy to pick up the pace and dragged Travis away from the creatures of the field.

"We have to save them," Travis said.

"Which ones?" Kane asked.

"All of them," Travis said.

"You sound like your father," Kane said.

Travis watched sadly as the fight continued, but sighed. He wished to know more about his parents, but he worried for the strange little creatures.

“Goodbye,” Travis called to them. “I will return if I can.”

“Donkey Butt, Donkey Butt,” they all sang in unison. “Tied with ropes! What a dope!” They laughed merrily.

“Hey,” Travis yelled at them. “Fine, off with the lot of you!”

They laughed and sang about him as Kane led him away. Once some time had passed, Travis, uncomfortable and looking to take his mind off the pain of being strapped to the Donk's rear end, broached the subject of his parents once more.

"What was my father like?" Travis asked.

"Your father was the most powerful being I'd ever seen," he said bluntly. "He was the last of his kind in this country. Few Elementals are still alive, and some are mere shadows of their formal glory."

"So my father made a sword for me?" Travis asked.

"No," Kane said. "Well, your mother made the sword part. Your father imbued it with vectory. It was a collaboration of both their talents. Your father was an otherworldly being, and your mother was a mechanical genius. You were their prized son, and your brother-"

"Brother?" Travis asked. This was the first he'd heard of having a brother.

"Ah, sorry," Kane stammered. "I did not mean to bring that up."

"I don't remember him," Travis murmured.

"That's probably for the best," Kane decided. "He likely suffered the same fate as your parents. Meaning he's either dead or..."

"Or what?" asked Travis.

"Travis," Kane said quietly. "The fire that started the night your parents died had a magical source. I believe something happened that caused your father to literally erupt in such an explosion of vectory that he burned down the cottage, taking himself, your mother, your brother, and the King with him. You were the sole survivor, Travis. And that makes you, one, an anomaly, and two, a person of interest for the royal family. My goal is to make sure you are prepared to defend yourself, should anyone, especially the Queen, force you to answer for your family's crimes. I believe you deserve a fair fight at least."

The enormity of these words hit Travis like a brick to his two front teeth. How could he, so lowly a worm, be so central to such intrigue? Kane laid it out so matter-of-factly, but the only fact that Travis cared about now was the suggestion that the Queen might have it out for him.

"I've been working with the Princess to secure your safe passage to the Clockwork Palace, but for now, we must acquire the sword your parents left you. It was confiscated at the scene of the fire the night your family died. The Princess and I believe there was some element of foul play. We do not hold your father responsible for murder without cause. The Queen is less predictable, so we must keep her in the dark on these matters. For reasons I will explain to you later, the power imbued within it may prove useful."

"So the Queen thinks my Dad killed the King?" Travis asked. "That's absolutely unhinged. I was better off in Mercy Square!"

"Travis, still thy tongue," said Kane. "It is best we keep our voices low."

"You've been blabbing on about this all afternoon," said Travis. "Now I'm tied to a donkey with a bounty on my head. Maybe it's better the Queen does catch me, because I don't know if I'm capable of defending myself from the most powerful woman in the country. What is this mad plan of yours, Kane?!"

Kane trotted a bit in silence, as if trying to suppress his temper. Travis's brain buzzed with information. *Did my dad really kill the King?*

"We should leave the country," Travis decided.

"We will," said Kane. "Once our business in Krankfert is complete. First we must acquire the sword, avoid the Queen, and strike down those villainous forces pooling on the horizon. After that, we'll have a wine and cheese party."

SOUTHERNER'S ROOST

After a day's ride they arrived at Southerner's Roost. It had been raining for a few hours. Travis, Kane, and Betsy were all exhausted. Travis's muscles felt like they might burst from the way that he'd been strapped to the Hover-Donk. He had to clench his entire body to keep from falling further face-forward into the donkey's butt. The sun was setting, but even the cover of nearing night and occasional thunder crashes could not shield Travis from the insults suddenly hurtling in his direction when the city were gates opened. Kane had plied the guardsmen by way of seeking shelter, but now that the guards had a look at these visitors, they'd crowded around with spears and shields at the ready.

"He's a Vec," cried a man in floppy green garb.

The townsfolk began peeking out their windows. Trapped inside by the storm, now all their eyes were focused on the scene at the gate. A man, dressed like a Vec, riding a clever-looking horse had entered their walls. With him was a floating metal animal, and strapped to its backside was a terrified boy.

An attractive young woman threw a handful of mud, striking Travis in the face. He struggled and protested. The woman shrieked in horror, having meant to hit Kane in the face but having missed badly. Betsy reared backward, frightened to be next, but in doing so caused Kane to lose his balance.

"Relent," cried Kane. "I am a member of the Royal Council."

The crowd murmured with suspicion. Some booed and howled.

The rain was pouring now. Visibility was scarce. There was no clear path for an exit. The crowd had surrounded them amidst the beating of the raindrops.

"I will speak only with Ducat Duncan himself," Kane said, trying to maintain his authority over the wary crowd.

An authoritative-looking knight came forward and addressed Kane.

"You are hereby under arrest for disturbance of the peace," he said. "And for suspicion of vectory. You will be kept in the dungeon until such time as you are either tried or executed depending on what Ducat Duncan decrees."

Kane protested. "I am an old friend of Ducat's. Please hear me out."

The snippy knight could not decide whether to trust Kane or not. The way Kane was dressed suggested vectory. But it had been said that the Queen kept a Vec on retainer to study their ways. It had been reported that the Queen's Vec had been stripped of his powers, but there was no way of confirming that this man wasn't lying his way inside the fort just to do something rotten to Ducat Duncan.

"Who are you exactly?" asked the guard. "And please provide identification."

Thunder crashed as Kane leapt from Betsy's back and retrieved his scroll, unfurling it at great length and booming with authority:

"I am Kane Verdalea, Chief Royal Historian of the Queen's Council, and as I've told you, a dear friend of Ducat's! What will Ducat think when one of his oldest and dearest friends has been kept out in the rain? He surely will be displeased. I mean to provide him with the greatest squire he's ever seen, and you mean to drown me in the Fates' bathwater? Have you no courtesy, man?!"

The knight sneered. He didn't want to be fooled by some ruse, but on the off-chance that Kane was telling the truth, he didn't want to receive Ducat's wrath. The other knights were unconvinced as well. They were eyeing Travis and asking one another if so scrawny a runt could survive Ducat's training.

"We shall discuss this in the stable," said the officious knight. "But if you are lying, know that you are walking into a lion's den. Be advised."

The officious knight turned and beckoned for them to follow, slipping a bit in the mud, shrugging, and marching away toward one of the outstretching arms of Ducat's fortress. The fort looked like a giant bird with two wings spreading toward the city gates. There were guards posted at sniping points along the walls, sticking their crossbows out of slits. It would be foolish to steal anything from such a place. Travis decided that he wanted no part of Kane's mad plan to steal the sword.

"Park your luggage here," the knight said, referring to the stables adjacent to the fort. Kane untied Travis. Travis clung to the Hover-Donk to make sure not to fall off the metal creature when he was finally released from his bindings.

In the reprieve of the stable's semi-leakproof overhanging, the knight in charge took stock of Travis, inspecting Kane's story for verity.

"Who is this wretch?" asked the guard, referring to Travis.

Travis disliked being called a wretch very much. The knight's classist tone reminded him of Vonkenschtook. Kane ignored this slight completely.

"He is a delinquent known for being a fierce fighter in the tavern circuit. I captured him after I found him drunk on guppers in a clearing. Apparently he had been trying to kiss the faeries of the fields and they inebriated him. Yes, he's a strong one alright, but dumb as a sack of rocks. He'll need Ducat's training if he's ever to make something of himself."

Travis was dumbfounded. Kane had invented for him an intricate backstory and had rambled through it so fast, Travis wasn't even certain he could remember it all. He tried to memorize it as quickly as possible, but soon realized that all of it hinged on him being an exceptional fighter. Aside from their harrowing escape from the jarters, Travis had no real fighting experience. Vonkenschtook had trained him to wield a stick like a sword, but beyond that he was hopeless.

"I fear if given to the prisons he will become a master of criminality, and so I give him to Ducat instead," Kane said.

"Strange mission from the Royal Council, recruiting local drunks for sale," said the knight, eyeing Kane like an intruder.

"This is a side-quest from my royal duties, I'll admit," Kane said. "I may be using it as a partial excuse to gain entrance to Ducat's museum. I am Chief Royal Historian and as such have a rather insatiable appetite for relics. I know Ducat has a treasure trove of them because I met him at the Princess's birthday celebration last year. He went on and on about it. I just had to see for himself."

The knight tilted his head back and forth. "Yes," he admitted. "He is quite partial to discussing his museum. Alright, I do believe you know the man."

Travis could tell that the guardsmen surrounding him were a bit disappointed by this decision. They were clearly aching for combat.

The knight led Kane and Travis through the gates at the east wing of the fortress. The hallway led to a banquet hall, which burst forth from its stem like a rose in bloom. The banquet table was thirty feet long with intricately carved benches along either side. There were enough place settings for a small army, but Travis reckoned that Ducat Duncan had more soldiers than settings, meaning these seats were only reserved for guests. At the head of the table there was a seat for Ducat Duncan emblazoned with a carving of Kamistrea, the Fate of laws and reason. Kamistrea was often depicted with four gigantic wings that could extend around the entirety of the world. It was said that the laws she made were the rules that governed everything. There was something beautiful about her stern yet reasonable face, thought Travis as he passed her carven visage.
Behind the table was a dual staircase that led up about twelve feet to Ducat Duncan's sizable throne. The throne seemed to be a relic, hard stone chiseled to resemble simple wood. On the throne sat Ducat Duncan, a mustached potato of a man adorned with a shock of red hair. He sat with his cheek indented on one set of knuckles, perching his whole head on his raised arm. He was an ornery man, and to those who knew him well, a threat.

"I remember you," called Ducat Duncan to Kane Verdalea.

"I remember you as well, my dear Ducat," called Kane.

"Flattery is time wasted," said Ducat. "What brings you here? Who is this wretch?"

Ducat was pointing at Travis. They had yet to settle themselves before the man, and here he was demanding answers. Ducat clearly had no time for pleasantries, even amongst old friends. The guards to Ducat's left and right, the crossbowmen perched along the balcony, and the anxiety they brought with them kept Travis quiet. *This is not what I expected,* Travis thought.

"A new recruit," said Kane, gesturing to Travis. "I was in the area to inspect some ruins. I'd heard tell that some villagers had complained about Vecs stealing children away in the night. While I was investigating, I came across this impish lad, whom I supposed might be an excellent candidate for your tutelage."

"Enough about the wretch," said Ducat. "On the matter of the ruins and the disappearances, there have been two missing women, one missing child, and one missing guardsman. My latest scouting party has not returned," said Ducat. "Tell me this, and be honest with me, Verdalea. Has the Queen herself sent you to investigate? Is this a matter of importance to the throne?"

"Yes," said Kane. "And by way of happenstance, I found this boy drunk in a field being kissed by oblings. He needs mentorship, guidance."

Travis shot Kane a hateful look.

"Do you see," said Kane, "the hatred in his eyes? He is a born fighter, but his brain is so swollen with ignorance that I fear he is beyond my help. Please train him."

"This is not a gift," said Ducat, sounding suddenly exhausted. "This is an obligation. Why must I take this wretch?"

"Stop calling me a wretch," said Travis.

The guards readied their weapons. Every crossbow in the building pointed at Travis. He froze.

"Look at that," said Kane, "and you'll see exactly why I've brought him before you. He's brave. A daring fool. He needs the guidance of a man of your stature and the leadership of your military. If anyone can make a knight out of this scoundrel it's Ducat Duncan. Or was that notion just a passing fancy?"

Ducat groaned and rolled his head around with exasperation.

"It is true," said Ducat. "My training course is rigorous. I force my recruits to eat nothing but cauliflower for forty days so that the bile and stupidity within them runs free. Then when they are empty inside, I instruct them to run laps around my labyrinth until they are limber and fit. Only then, when they are instilled with fortitude by my regimen, may they face the peril that awaits them inside."

This sounded like madness to Travis, something far worse than even Vonkenschtook could concoct. What was Kane thinking bringing Travis here?

"Yes, well," Kane said, adjusting his spectacles. "I certainly don't question your methods. I merely request that you give the boy a fair shake."

Ducat sighed. "Very well, Verdalea."

"Then it's settled," said Kane. "Now if I might trouble you for an additional favor."

"Taking this stringy whelp is your favor," said Ducat. “Have you no shame?”

"Some, but not nearly enough to stay silent, I’m afraid," said Kane. "And do not underestimate the whelp’s abilities. He is a clever lad in spite of his low nature. After all, he rose to prominence in the gang fights of Clockwork City. Those are not for the weak. They called him the Rat-Catcher. It was said that he could strike a man in the throat so forcefully the man’s head would explode."

Ducat stood upright and grabbed Travis hard by the shoulder, inspecting him closely with foul breath that came out panting like a dog’s.

“Yes,” Ducat said, surveying Travis’s face carefully. “There is something odd in his eyes, I’ll give you that.”

Travis wriggled his chin free of Ducat’s grasp, growling.

“Rebellion is the fire of youth,” said Ducat, wiping his hand on a kerchief from his pocket. “With training and discipline it can be snuffed out forever.”

There was a moment when Ducat and Travis’s eyes locked. Such vehement contempt was shared between them that the room fell deadly silent.

"Let us speak of something pleasant,” Kane said. "I overheard while dining at the palace that your museum is the jewel of southern Krankfert.”

This bit of gossip sidetracked Ducat from his contempt.

"They speak of my treasures at the palace, do they? Well, perhaps I should show you my prizes, piece-by-piece. Then you could share firsthand the beauty you beheld to all you encounter on your travels."

Ducat whistled for the knight who'd led them inside the fortress.

"Kingston," said Ducat, addressing the knight by name. "Take this new recruit to the barracks and have him stuffed with cauliflower."

"Yes, my lord," said Kingston, grabbing Travis by the arm and dragging him down the stairs from the throne platform to the dining hall below.

"Wait," said Kane, calling after Kingston. "I realize this must come across as rather presumptuous, but I would like to show the Rat-Catcher your treasures as well."

Ducat shuddered and made a guttural sound of disgust. "Blech," he said. "To think of one so low amongst artifacts so hallowed. Highly repellent."

"Precisely my point," said Kane, his eyes lighting up with glee. "I have a theory that I have been concocting for a year's time. I believe in the power of art, as well as you do, to elevate the mind and instill nobility in the onlooker. I hypothesize that in showing immaculate works of beauty to a wretch like this, we shall expand his mind and motivate him to fight even harder. What is life without motivation? If all he knows is scum, than his behavior will surely match. But give him a taste of glamor..."

Ducat rubbed his puffy fingers against his mustache. "I see your supposition clearly now," he mused. "You believe a taste of treasure might motivate him to make something of himself. A bold proposition, Verdalea. In truth, the success of my army may well be attributed to such an effect."

"I'm so glad you agree," said Kane. "Who knows how many of your men have been motivated to fight harder for Southerner's Roost knowing the splendor of the treasures housed within these walls? They may be living proof of my theory."

"Yes," said Ducat. "Of course I am willing to be the subject of any academic writings on beauty or nobility."

"Yes, of course," Kane replied. "But let us use this lowly wretch as a test case, shall we? Should he see the museum and survive your trials, he will be proof that art can inspire even the lowliest of scum."

Travis was uncertain whether to be more upset by Kane's use of the word "scum" or his suggestion that Travis might not survive Ducat's training. Before he could decide, Ducat stood up and proclaimed:

"Take him to the treasury at once! Let me guide him myself! Come, Verdalea! We shall prove to Krankfert that my treasures could inspire even the lowliest rat!"

Ducat marched past Kane and ripped Travis free from Kingston's clutches. Now Ducat was dragging Travis by the collar through the dining hall and to the adjacent corridor where the treasury was located. Kane scampered down the stairway after them with Kingston and a coterie of guardsmen following behind.

Ducat led them down another hallway toward a locked room with a gilded door. From around his neck he procured a key dangling on the end of a chain. The key, like the door, was golden. He inserted the key into the lock. With a sizable *CLICK* the door unlocked. There seemed to be a mechanism further inside the door that connected to gears within it like a machine. Travis winced at the sound of the door clanking and shuddering. The door swung forth swung forth suddenly, as if pulled by a poltergeist. An elderly guardsman caught the door as it swung forth, acting as a human doorstopper. He exerted himself greatly and groaned with pain.

Once the door swung open, Ducat ushered them all inside, whereupon Travis spied the most glittering collection of prizes he'd ever laid eyes upon. His dreams of seeing the Clockwork City had been replaced in an instant with a new visage of royalty, beauty, and luxury.

Inside Ducat Duncan's Treasure Room were cases upon cases of ornate, immaculate statues, necklaces with jeweled amulets, tiaras, headdresses, scepters, weapons from historic wars- including the onyx axe from the Grimalkin Entanglement- and the remnants of an Elemental font. It was a thief's dream.

"This here, Verdalea," said Ducat, gesturing toward one case in particular, "was the actual amulet worn by Zounds Mantis on the day she slaughtered Milosch the Mighty. Some days I wish we could return to those times, when we could destroy every Vec on sight. When their bones are tossed into the sea, when their ashes are scattered to the four winds, only then will the tension in my heart subside."

There was an awkward silence. Travis eyed Kane for a sense of how he was supposed to feel. Here was an avowed defender of the kingdom, speaking about his dreams of genocide. Seemingly realizing the reason for the silence, especially given the amount of guardsmen surrounding them, Ducat spoke suddenly.

"Not you, Verdalea. The others I mean. I know you have taken great steps to eradicate the toxins within you."

He walked away to another case. *So it was less a threat and more a poor turn of phrase?* Travis wondered if Ducat was truly as cruel as he seemed.

That was when Travis's eyes met the sword. It was glistening in the center of the room. It was held upright with its immaculate fate-stone blade aimed at the Fates themselves, as if posing a threat to any who might try to upset it. There was a cloudiness where the blade met the hilt as if the sword were enchanted. Three mesmerizing gemstones rested in the hilt as well. Travis was awestruck.

Beyond the obvious monetary value, there seemed to be something spiritually calling out to Travis from the blade like it was vaguely sentient. He sensed that a presence- one he knew well- was alive within the blade, trapped within its vectory. Travis turned his eyes to Kane, who averted his own and returned to Ducat.

Ducat sighed and moved toward the sword. He approached the case with consternation, placing his puffy pink fingers on the glass.

"This of course was the sword made by the traitor Elaina and her husband Alfonse Sebastian. I keep it here because of its beauty, but also because it is a grim reminder of what may happen to traitors. Elaina burned to ash, along with her husband Alfonse, but damn them both, they took the King with them."

Ducat pounded his fist against the case. Travis tried to hide the rage he felt on behalf of his family. When he shot a look of determination toward Kane, he was surprised to find that Kane was staring back at him.

"You know," Kane said, "it is said there was a survivor."

Ducat raised a furry eyebrow to Kane's assertion.

"They say that the survivor was the reason for the fire," Kane said. "The King arrived unexpectedly, wishing to surprise his old friends. Then he saw that they had one more child than they'd previously mentioned, and there was something strange about that child. Have you heard that, Ducat?"

"Absolute nonsense," said Ducat. "If this unverifiable rumor were even remotely possible there would be a shred of evidence to back it up, but here you are telling me, the absolute authority on history in this region that you know better! Well!"

"I am Chief Historian as appointed by the Crown," said Kane. "And I know more of magic-related matters than most, wouldn't you say?"

"That may be true," said Ducat. "But it is surely a dark mark on your record rather than something worth bragging about, Verdalea. Remember where you are!"

The guards were back at the ready, all weapons pointed at Kane.

"Matters of the crown outweigh city matters," suggested Kane.

"More poppycock," said Ducat. "I will not hear of spells and sorcery. You are in a city of human law. A man's bones and muscle determine his fate, not his ability to torment particles in the air. It is because of your past as a Vec that I detest you, Verdalea. Otherwise I might like to be friends."

"Ehh," said Kane. "Yes, well, that would be fine, but my business here is merely transactional. I must inspect the nearby ruins where locals have gone missing."

"Yes," said Ducat. "I do not trifle in magical matters."

Travis inched closer to the sword. As he approached it, he swore he could hear his mother's voice singing from within the blade. He wanted to place his hands upon the glass, see if it would trigger anything, but as soon as he reached toward the case Kingston shouted at him.

"Rat-Catcher," called Kingston. "Away from that!"

"That was to be expected," said Ducat. "But it is no concern to me. My cases are reinforced glass. See the way the gilding slinks along the edges of the glass? This is clever artistry. In fact those same golden leaves keep the glass wedged firmly in place, bound to the ground around us. There is truly no removing it, no matter how skilled a thief may be. But please, keep the wretch from dirtying the glass."

"I'd wager the only blade strong enough to smash the glass is the sword itself," said Kane. "That's quite the predicament."

"You trouble me with your riddles," said Ducat. "I believe you have spent enough time surveying my treasures."

Ducat ushered Kane out of the museum suddenly, as if he had become suspicious. Kane tried not to take offense, and bowed.

"I thank you for blessing me with a tour," said Kane. "I find that a person of my curiosity could spend hours in a museum such as this, but to be granted a few moments in yours has been a rare pleasure."

Ducat blushed.

"Yes, well, it has been an honor, indeed," he said.

Kingston butted Travis in the back of the head with his spear and ushered him out the door. It was clear that if Travis wanted to inspect the sword further, he would need to get as far away from Kingston as possible.

Ducat, Kane, Kingston and Travis left the room and entered the long hallway outlining the dining room and leading toward the fort's main entrance. Kane paused as if to say a few final words.

"Rat-Catcher," Kane said to Travis. "Learn well what the knights have to offer. You may be the strongest where you come from, but there is a wide world beyond the sewers you know and love. As for you, Kingston, was it? Try not to treat the poor wretch unkindly. He means well. Perhaps you can show him the fundamentals of combat, decency, how not to spit in public, et cetera."

Kingston took the words like a mountain receiving rain.

"Ducat, thank you again for your hospitality. Should you need me, I shall be inspecting the ruins to the north. On behalf of the Queen, good day," said Kane.

He turned to leave, but Ducat's arm shot out and grabbed him. Kane turned with a glint of fear in his eyes. He had not been expecting any complications.

"Be wary, Verdalea," said Ducat. "Those ruins... there is something truly amiss. Under the brightness of the moon, I've heard strange screeches."

Kane nodded, seemingly shaken by Ducat's words.

"I will take the highest precautions," said Kane, freeing himself from Ducat's grip and preparing to leave. "Farewell, Ducat."

Kane turned without so much as glancing at Travis and quickly trotted away toward the fort's exit.

"Wait," Travis shouted.

He could see Kane stumble slightly, but after a pause he rounded the corner. He was gone. He had truly left Travis. He had adopted him and abandoned him.

Travis was immediately butted in the back of the head by Kingston's spear.

"Do not speak in the great Ducat's presence, whelp!"

Ducat gestured to Travis, ordering Kingston to take care of him.

"New meat," Ducat said. "Get this cur away from me.”

Kingston grabbed Travis and dragged him down a staircase into the dungeon. Travis fumbled and gasped as Kingston dragged him. Kingston shrugged him off, causing him to fall. Kingston yanked him upright. At the bottom, Kingston tossed him into a doorway with loud cackling on the other side.

The next room was a private pub for Ducat’s knights. The knights inside were raving drunk. They played games and gambled and told bawdy stories and laughed uncontrollably. Travis had never seen anything like it. *Debauchery*, he thought.

They all stopped and looked at Travis when he entered. He was clearly new, and they were ready to pounce at the first sign of weakness.

"This wretch comes before us," said Kingston, "in hopes of joining our order. Shall we welcome him with open arms?"

"No," the knights cried, standing in unison. "With these arms!"

They raised their weapons and cheered hellishly. Travis was petrified, but he tried to scowl indifferently. He knew that to show fear might mean death.

"Then it is decided," said Kingston. "There is no brotherhood between us! We shall forgo the normal training and proceed with the only proof necessary to separate a knight from a wretch and a wretch from his life. But there is honor in combat! Should he prove himself worthy, we shall welcome him with open arms."

The knights cheered drunkenly.

"Send him to the labyrinth!"

DEATH SENTENCE

Another knight sounded a bell, and suddenly bells began gonging from all around Travis. The entire town was being alerted.

Death, Travis thought. *This is a death sentence.*

He needed to fight his way free. He tried for the door behind him, but a pair of knights were already blocking the way. Two of the brutes grabbed Travis by either arm and dragged him screaming into the corridor.

Deeper and deeper they traveled underneath the fortress until there was a glinting at the far end of a tunnel. Torch fires burned proudly around what seemed to be another castle built beneath the fortress. Its large stone walls became visible when Travis was pulled through the darkened passageway into the wider broader area beyond. It was a chamber that seemed to be the size of a city itself. There were stone benches built into the walls above. Travis was in awe of the place's grandeur.

The knights began snickering when they saw Travis's surprise. Kingston spoke to him softly.

"Do not gape at it like a Grimalkin," Kingston hissed. "Stand and fight."

Travis blinked suddenly, realizing what he was meant to do.

"Come," said one of the stockier mustached knights. "This one's sure to die at the spikes. Let's at least give him a fighting chance."

Kingston clucked his tongue.

There were townspeople gathering in the balcony above, traveling down steep staircases to their seats. They were so high above Travis that they looked like insects, little ricticks scrambling for a feast.

The entirety of Ducat Duncan's army had followed Travis down into the tunnels. He had an escort of at least one hundred and seventy men, all in full armor, armed to the teeth.

"Ready to meet the Fates firsthand?" asked one of the knights.

Some of the others laughed. Travis tried to shake the fear out of his head.

"Never trust a stranger," Vonkenschtook's voice echoed in Travis's memory. "A stranger's word is only as good as what he can get from you."

In spite of the source, Vonkenschtook's words rang true. What Travis thought Vonkenschtook had meant was that you cannot know for certain a stranger's intentions. Their words could be a lie, even if they appear to be kind. Their words could be true, even when they are devastating. Without knowing the person delivering the information, it is impossible to say for certain that they have your best interests at heart. So there was always equal potential for a stranger to say something that seemed true, simply because they were strange.

The knights began thumping the butt-end of their spears against the dirt below, snapping Travis back to reality. From a nearby passageway, Ducat Duncan rode a great chocolate stallion toward Travis.

"It seems my knights have rejected your application to join our guardsmen," Ducat said to Travis. "No matter. If you are truly as adept a fighter as Kane Verdalea says then you shall have no difficulty proving yourself in my labyrinth."

Ducat spoke as though Travis had some choice in the matter. He'd simply been duped by Kane into this situation. Before Travis could muster up the words to defend himself, Ducat rode past him and addressed his knights.

"Knights of Southerner's Roost! Prepare for this wretch a costume of sorts. Not our finest armor, but what have we to spare? Such will be given to him, as such he is worth. Born without nobility, living off the dregs of humanity, this scum represents all who have fallen beyond the law's help. It is our sworn duty as Knights of Southerner's Roost to protect our city from such villainy."

The knights cheered.

"Let me go," said Travis. "I'll- I'll tell the Princess you were cruel to me!"

The knights laughed at him.

"If you are worthy of redemption," Ducat said. "Prove your worth by besting my challenges. And if you fail it is no matter. You will not be the first child to die within these walls. Throw him inside, and the let the challenge begin!"

Ducat rode away, around the outer rim of the arena, obscured from Travis's view.

The knights had found an old chamber pot and a heavy cuirass that had all but rusted to disrepair. They slid the cuirass over Travis's body. It nearly forced him to the ground with its weight. They laughed and slapped the chamber pot on his head. They found a training sword, an old wooden toy, and gave him that to defend himself. They righted him and shoved him toward the doors, gathering around him so he had no escape. Two of the men unbarred the doors and opened them.

Travis saw a long stone hallway that turned sharply to the right. There were metal fixtures jutting out from either wall, two on one side and one on the other. There was a circular hole in each one, about the size of a human head. Before Travis could get a better sense of what he was looking at, Kingston shoved Travis inside the labyrinth.

TRAVIS & THE LABYRINTH

Travis stumbled forward. There would be no escape now. The men barred the doors behind him. Then from above, the people of Southerner's Roost roared. Travis fell to his knees under the weight of the armor. He removed the chamber pot, inspected it, then tossed it aside. He slinked out of his armor like a turtle removing its shell. Then he gazed upward at the ring of spectators around him. They were a writhing cascade of colors. He could barely make out individual faces. They seemed so small to him, yet their presence loomed so large. He was used to being secluded in the orphanage, not being the center of attention. Now an arena's worth of people were focusing their gaze on him. His jaw tightened so hard he felt as though his teeth might shatter. His breath quickened. He could feel his heartbeat pounding against his temples. The crowd howled at him.

"RAHHHHHHHHHHHHHH!"

It was the loudest he'd ever shouted in his life. They were so far away that he wasn't even sure if they could hear him, but they could not harm him either. He was alone to face whatever challenges the labyrinth held. The knights were locked behind the door now, and it was unlikely they would come chasing after him.

They don't know what I have been through already, he thought.

A weaker child, a more coddled or spoiled one, might have chosen to stay put, to beat against the door and beg for mercy, but not Travis. He decided right then that he would soldier on, against whatever challenges were ahead. He knew from his connection to the sword that Kane had been telling at least some version of the truth, which meant if he wanted to understand more about his parents, he would need to defeat the labyrinth. He vowed that he would discover the truth about the sword and his family, even if it meant he would face death.

I've already faced Vonkenschtook, Travis thought.

Travis felt a weight being lifted, and not just because the rusty cuirass was now laying at his feet. Should he survive, it would be by his own merit. And should he fail, it would be the result of his own stupidity. His wits were his only defense.

This is the adventure you've always dreamed of, he told himself.

As he worked up the nerve to march forward, a grinding mechanical sound erupted from the walls. Long cylindrical beams slid forth, creating a zig-zag path between Travis and the end of the hallway. The beams bristled with spines like a jarter's tail. They were mechanical in nature and their barbs, metal spikes coated in oil, rotated threateningly. What had once been a clear path now was a treacherous series of traps. The crowd hooted at him like he was destined to fail.

Travis surveyed the twisted pegs, scanning them for safe passage. There had to be some means of crossing them, or else none of the other knights would have passed this test and joined Ducat's legion. To touch any of these barbed spikes could mean a severe wound, what with the way they were twirling, and the oil that coated the barbs might infect or burn like a snapworm bite. Travis had to be cautious.

Think of something clever if you really are so clever, he told himself.

Travis noticed that the first log did not reach the exact end of the opposite wall. He would be able to sneak past it if he was careful, so long as he was mindful of the individual longer spikes on either beam. Spikes jutted out of the beams at random but the order in which they spun could be memorized. This meant Travis could plan when to make his moves. He crouched, trying to make himself small, hoping to be nimble enough to sneak between the logs. With a careful leap Travis dodged between the spinning barbs and hunkered against the wall behind him. Now he was between the first and second logs, contorted in such a way that no barbs would strike him during their normal rotations. Though uncomfortable, he was able to survey the next part of the challenge.

There were two long barbs in the exact center of his path. One sprang from the closer log, another from the further log, so that they might strike him at the same time as he passed. If he timed his journey correctly, he would be able to miss them both, but if he failed to cross in time he would be ripped apart.

Travis tried to force a sense of calmness within him so he would not panic. There was a point when he saw it, felt it within himself, a centered moment of wonder. He could feel his body moving before it began, sense that its timing was perfect. The logs seemed to slow down, the barbs barely twitching. He was focused now.

Chik-Chik-Chik. Now!

He ran. He ran with all his might and slid across the dirt as the twin barbs sailed past him. When he slapped his palms against the wall to stop his momentum he laughed. He'd made it. He hadn't even felt the journey when it happened. His mind had just flashed white and he'd arrived. The crowd roared.

He looked back over his shoulder and there were the barbs, still rotating as threateningly as ever. He had just enough room to sneak past the second log, leaving only the third one in his way.

Now that he could see it clearly, Travis understood the joke of the whole situation. The final log stretched the entire width of the hall. There was no passage between the log and the wall. Travis was trapped.

He panicked and started eyeing the log for an opening, but there were too many barbs. To even chance it could mean death.

The armor, he thought. But it was heavy, cumbersome and now on the other side of the first log where he'd left it. He moaned and grabbed at his own hair. The crowd laughed at him, recognizing his trepidation even from a distance. Travis could hear them thundering in his head.

HE'S STUCK! HE'S TOO STUPID TO FIGURE IT OUT!

Travis growled with sudden determination.

In order to cross the third log, Travis would need to go back between the two logs he'd just passed, grab the armor, and while he was at it, grab the bedpan and the sword, then head back through the barbs again, newly encumbered, and *then* cross the third log. It was a slog, but Travis had little choice.

The timing would be different from this side. He would have to pause for a moment while the logs completed a full rotation. If he ran straight ahead, the barbs would spiral and kill him.

So he lunged past the first set of barbs as they passed, then stopped suddenly, nearly stumbling forward and getting a face full of death. The crowd cheered for blood, but he was safe. The barbs twiddled like ricktick antennae in front of his nose. He waited for them to circle around again, and began breathing slowly. There was something about the slow breathing that calmed him. He could pace out and measure the breath like he was measuring time, slowing it to a crawl.

He rushed past the barbs again, stopping before striking the other wall, then sidling past the first log easily and hobbling back toward the rusty cuirass that was laying in the dirt before him. He threw it over his body once more, moaning a bit with discomfort. Then, stopping a moment before heading back toward the barbs, he snagged the bedpan from off the ground and placed it atop his head.

Travis could hear them howling with laughter. He smirked. He imagined that the image probably did look a bit funny. There he was a scrawny lad in an oversized busted up chest piece with a receptacle for human waste on his head.

At least it was clean when they gave it to me, he thought.

He plucked the wooden sword from the dirt where he'd dropped it. He tried to head back toward the spinning barbs, but he was much too slow in the heavy cuirass. It would take all his strength to get up to speed while wearing the thing. It was so big on him that it rose to his mouth.

Travis rushed forward, and he could see himself fail. He would clear the first barb, but he felt a bit too tall for the longer one on his left.

As he slid under it, the second barb smacked him right in the bedpan, and the chamber pot flipped off and landed on the ground behind him. Travis rested in the dead spot between the barbs and crouched, trying to regain his breath. The crowd gasped when they saw the chamber pot fly off, thinking it was the boy's head.

Travis grabbed the chamber pot and dove forward, landing on the breast of his armor, wooden sword lurching outright.

He rolled onto his side with a groan. In spite of the pain, the hop had worked. He was clear of the first log again. He just needed to sidle carefully past the second and find a way past that treacherous third one.

As he shuffled upright against the wall, he studied the pattern between the second and third log as best he could. It seemed as though there was a long bare patch in the center of the third log, but the spikes at its ends were long and sharp, giving Travis little time to climb over or under them before the spikes came around again. He would not be able to climb over the log quickly while wearing the cuirass.

He jutted his wooden training sword against the spikes, but the wooden sword snapped. A huge part of it cracked off, leaving it little more than a wooden dagger.

"It's too flimsy," Travis said.

He inspected the hinged shoulder plates on his cuirass, and sure enough, one was damaged. He removed the armor and promptly bashed off one of the shoulder plates with the bedpan. Taking the shattered shard of armor he wedged the curved metal of the shoulder plate into the space between the log and the wall. He jammed it in hard, and the machine creaked and shuddered, unable to turn.

It would be easy for Travis to cross now, as the bare spot on the third log was frozen in place. Travis donned the cuirass once more, put the chamber pot atop his head, and tossed his flimsy wooden dagger over the side of the log. Surveying his options, Travis confirmed that it might be best to go over the log rather than under it. The spikes on the opposite end were pointed down, so he would have better luck crossing them should the machine start spinning again. Speaking of which, it seemed to be jittering a bit more now. Travis saw the shoulder plate slowly sliding out of place from where he'd wedged it. Any more motion and the machine could start again!

No time to think! Travis thought.

Travis pulled himself with all his might over the log, just as the shoulder plate broke and the machine sprang back to life. As he leapt and landed, the spikes on the other side of the log came soaring round and sliced against the pack part of his armor. Travis howled in agony and fell forward, certain he'd been fatally wounded. He clawed at the dirt in front of him, gasping for breath. As his eyes closed, he thought of the Princess. A few seconds later he realized that he wasn't in pain. The spike had indeed scratched Travis's armor quite fiercely, but it had failed to penetrate the metal. He was unharmed.

He checked himself for wounds, stepping forward, out of the device's range. But there was no blood, only some scratches on the armor where it had saved him. He had been right to take it with him after all. Bending over, Travis plucked the shattered wooden dagger off the dirt. From that point onward, Travis decided to treasure all of the gifts the Fates provided him, however lowly they seemed. With that resolution he rounded the first corner of the labyrinth.

DAMSEL & DISTRESS

Around the corner there was a strange sight. Rather than a long deep maze like Travis had been imagining, there was instead a shallow recess with a stone hearth at the center of it adorned by four black birds clutching at a strange sculpture in the center, a skull with twin horns. There were roses lodged in the skull's teeth.

At the sight of him, the crows began shrieking. Travis froze in fear, eyeing them. Eight black unblinking eyes stared back. One of the crows had a tuft of grey on its leg and a villainous intellect. It spread its wings and flapped a little, rubbing its compatriots across the chest. The crows stopped moving. They watched Travis silently, never seeming to blink.

Perhaps they only eat when people die, Travis thought.

His heartbeat quickened and he found himself in a cold sweat.

They did not move, did not tilt their heads, did not pick at their feathers or flutter. They sat silently still, gargoyles if not for the glimmer of hunger.

Travis took a deep breath and tried to freeze the look of fear on his face. *They can scare me, but they can't predict what I'm thinking. And I'm smarter than a bird, aren't I?* Even though he wasn't convinced, he hatched a plan.

In front of him, under the crows, was a small hole. It was built to resemble the back part of a fireplace. Travis would have no difficulty crawling through the hole because of his small stature, but then there was the matter of the crows perched overhead. Perhaps they were trained to attack those who crawled through. Before the small recess containing the skulls, the crows and the crawlspace, there was another hallway that stretched to Travis's left and right. He darted suddenly in one direction, hoping to catch the crows off guard. He heard no sound at all.

In this direction there was another hallway stretching side-to-side. Before him on the floor the stones were marked with blue X's, except for one around the corner which was marked with a big red O. Further along, atop a small staircase, was a delicate maiden. The maiden wore a garland of fire-petals in her auburn hair. Her hair was long and flowed past her shoulders. She wore a silken white dress with lots of ruffles. There were scarves that stretched around her forearms.

"Oh, brave and noble warrior," she said. "You have come to me at last, have you? Please, rescue me from this horrid maze and I shall give you my favor!"

Travis had no idea what she meant, so he stayed completely still. He remembered the strange markings on the floor. All the stone slabs in this hallway had blue X's on them, except for the slab immediately in front of the maiden, which had a big red O on it. Perhaps it simply meant that the maiden was a prize.

But hang on, Travis thought. *If the floor was built with her in mind it might mean that she is one of the labyrinth's traps.*

He plucked the bedpan from off his head and removed his cuirass. Putting the bedpan back on, he heaved the rusty cuirass across the slab in front of him, tossing it on the big red 'O'. As soon as it clattered against the ground, the slab below it split in half and gave way, revealing a pit with spears below, their points gleaming amidst ruddy broadhead edges. Travis's rusty cuirass tumbled down upon them, skewering itself awkwardly between two of them, a clear sign of Travis's would-be fate had he made the mistake of rushing toward the maiden.

"Oh-ho," she shouted. "Somebody's clever."

Leaning her shoulders and mountain of hair against the stone wall behind her, the maiden unfastened something from amongst her many scarves and aimed it toward Travis's chest. He felt an instinctive urge to run. He dove to his left side quickly, just as the woman fired a bolt from her crossbow.

Travis breathed heavily, having slightly knocked the wind out of his own sails in landing so hard on his abdomen. The bases of his palms were scuffed and chapped, aching now, ready to ooze with blood.

"Coward," she called after him. "Face me like a true knight!"

She'd missed him, and it didn't sound as though she was coming after him either. *She can't,* he realized. *To step forward from her perch would mean to cross the spiky pit.* Her attire was too cumbersome.

Travis smiled. Bad luck was lurking around every corner.

He crossed back toward the first intersection, shaken.

The crows were cawing loudly like vile laughter. He passed them by and went in the opposite direction, toward the only remaining hallway. They shut up suddenly, as if shocked that he hadn't noticed them. He had of course, but he wasn't about to let those winged vermin have the satisfaction of knowing it.

There was a sharp turn to the left, then another long hall. Travis walked down it slowly and uncertainly. He couldn't believe how close he'd come to death. If that crossbow bolt had struck him in the head or heart...

He took a hard left and found a wall. He patted it for secrets, any sort of hidden indentation. He grunted. This entire right hallway seemed to be a dead end. This meant the only path forward was through the fireplace under the crows.

He sighed and stretched. At least this was a moment of solitude.

CLUNK-A-LUNKA-LUNK.

From the corner behind him a series of gears and levers groaned to life. Travis froze. There was something very wrong. He heard hot breathing. The crowd was chanting something. There was a cage in front of him now where the wall used to be. They'd rotated the wall out of view and replaced it with *Ja-Jaguar, Ja-Jaguar.* The iron bars of the cage swung open and the creature stepped forward, already stalking its prey.

TRAPPED LIKE A RAT

In what might have been his final thought, Travis realized the cleverness of the maze. Ducat Duncan had not struck him as a clever man. Rather he had seemed a sadist. Perhaps pushed by his own passion for building an army of superb fighters, Ducat had surpassed even his own mind's natural inclination toward dullness and designed this hellish labyrinth.

Travis had been lulled into a feeling of security by the dead end, the only area in this part of the labyrinth without any threats. Ducat had anticipated this and placed the creature in such a fashion that it would spring upon him as soon as he reached the dead end, meaning it had trapped him between the wall and the exit.

Ja-Jaguar, Ja-Jaguar, the crowd chanted.

Travis could see particles of dirt hanging in the air. The eyes of the glinting creature before him seemed to be irradiating a blinding light that disabled him from getting a clear look at anything beyond its fangs. His body loosened, and he could not feel himself breathing, as if the organs within him had slowed their own pulsating to find kinship with the world around them. There was something caressing his cheek like a mother urging him not to have fear. Travis could taste his own death, old and murky, hanging like mud in the air. He took a deep breath, and somehow, in doing so, had broken this spell.

Time pecked impetuously at the inside of its egg.

Ka-Chunk.

The wall had finished closing completely. The cage slid open. He could see the beast step forward. *Ja-Jaguar* they had called it.

The body was that of a wolf but the face was a cat's. The spines on its back appeared to be a mix of rock and metal ore, as if the creature was made of the earth itself. Its eyes were piercing white, emitting steam and black oil tears when it blinked. The tears ran down its ruddy-orange cheeks into the white parts of its tufted beard, coating it and recoating it with slime that ran down into the black edges of its low-hanging lips. Its white eyes steaming and its lips curling back ravenously, it was snuffling at the air, licking at its own tears.

How can it even see with eyes like that? Travis wondered.

There was no time to think. Ja-Jaguar lurched toward him, swiping at him with a paw tipped with jagged rocks. Travis fell backward. That was when the beast leapt upon him, lurching outward with both sets of claws.

His fingers deftly grabbed the rung of his bedpan and held it forward like a shield, clanging the thing against Ja-Jaguar's steaming face. The rocky cat's arms sailed past Travis on either side, clawing at the walls and dirt. Travis leapt over the cat's stunned body and ran as fast as he could in the opposite direction.

"Gaaahrrl," Ja-Jaguar howled with pain.

It shook its head violently as if sneezing out the discomfort. It roared and stampeded back toward Travis, chasing him around the corner into the longer hallway. As it called "*GAR GAR GAR!*"

it shot rocky spines out of its back, creating a volley of spears that landed before Travis, blocking his path.

"Gar, gar, gar," it said playfully as it heard him claw at the spines and whine.

It stalked ever closer.

As Travis tried to right himself over the rocky spines, they dug into his ribs and cut at him. One spine split beneath him, and he fell backward onto the ground. Ja-Jaguar was a few yards away now. It leapt, plunging down like an arrow upon Travis, and just like that, Travis grabbed the broken spike that had split beneath him and shot it upward into Ja-Jaguar's ribs. Travis released the spine, as Ja-Jaguar howled and sputtered. It tried to speak but could not emit the words.

The creature fell upon him, but its vitality was fleeting. Travis was pinned to the ground, wrapped in its bleeding body. Ja-Jaguar slumped over and bled, breathing slowly. Travis scrambled to pull himself out from under the heavy cat.

It blinked at him, the steam gone, but the oily tears still pouring. *No, they seemed to be slowing now*, he thought, as if they too were draining away, depleting along with its life force. Travis wanted to cry, wanted to look away, but he forced himself to accept the act. *I needed to do it to survive.*

The spear that had pierced the creature's heart had been a spine from its own back, but Travis had driven the blade into the beast. He was a killer, cold and hard, and now, he would watch it bleed out slowly, resigned to his fate.

Travis recalled his own torture in Vonkenschtook's basement. *If I had known I was to die, it would have been kinder to put me out of my misery.*

Gently he knelt before the creature. He nodded resolutely.

"I'm sorry," he said. "You were going to kill me. We're all trapped, trying to survive. If there had been another way, I would have taken it."

Mournfully the creature blinked and breathed. Travis inhaled and pulled the spine from Ja-Jaguar's side. Ja-Jaguar groaned in a mixture of anguish and relief, seeming to sink into the earth itself, more a pile of rocky rubble than a creature any longer. *It truly is vectory,* Travis thought. *And it does not seem evil. My heart tells me that this is a good creature, ruined by this foul place.*

FOUR CROWS

Ja-Jaguar's spirit erupted into a tiger-colored ghost that exploded and rushed upward toward the crowd in a series of swirling screeches. The crowd shrieked in horror, some stepping over each other to avoid being touched by its vectory.

Travis backed away compulsively, frightened to have upset the creature further. But as he righted himself, he saw no further movement in the creature's corpse. Ja-Jaguar was lifeless. Travis shuddered and turned back toward the crows. Yes, they would be waiting for him on that strange antlered hearth. He'd have to deal with them somehow. But after facing the last two challenges, and now knowing he only had one way forward, he felt solidly resolved to accomplish whatever he could. He had come too far already. But when he turned the corner and spied the hearth, he saw something that shocked him.

There were no crows.

This initially seemed like good news, but it also seemed very suspicious. The crows had seemed clever, especially the one with the grey spot.

Perhaps they are feeding on Ja-Jaguar? It was too awful to consider. He timidly crept forward toward the hearth, so he could clearly see through the small tunnel to the other side of the maze. The path was clear, and he could see a rope hanging in the hallway beyond. He sighed and got down on his hands and knees and began to crawl. The ground seemed solid enough. He grunted as he crawled his way through, hoping he hadn't overlooked another deadly puzzle.

In front of Travis was another hallway, but in the center there was a rope attached to an overhanging beam. The rope had been rigged mechanically to swing in a circular motion around a muddy pit below. In the pit there were toxic eels known as noxia, a type of mud-dwelling fish that fed on rats, lizards, and low-flying birds, renowned for stunning their prey by emitting a toxic gas from their heads.

As Travis stood up and inspected the rope and pit of death, an inhuman voice rasped behind him. *KAHHHHH,* it bellowed. It was coming from beyond the tunnel. Travis crouched to get a look into the hearth. He saw Ja-Jaguar's corpse staring back at him, now controlled like a puppet by some cruel twist of vectory. *Ja-Jaguar* was a thoughtless monster now, contorted, its bones out of sort, its form a writhing zombie, with an aura of madness and chaos about it, as if whatever spirit had erupted from its corpse had been replaced with the corrupting force torturing it. The poison had taken over now.

Travis backed away, and heard the chittering, shaking, vibrating of the eels in the mud behind him. He was trapped once more, between the pit of poisonous water-snakes and an undead creature. Ja-Jaguar's corpse growled and shambled forward, its legs looking out of joint, bending the wrong ways as they dragged its body.

Travis could barely blink. He had only enough time to make one solid jump for the rope, but he hadn't studied its rotation very carefully.

"*KAAAAAAAH!*" said Ja-Jaguar.

Ja-Jaguar's flesh erupted with black-and-white ringed vectory. Ja-Jaguar stretched forward on bewitched spider legs and slashed at Travis, trying to spear him. He backed his heels toward the pit and turned, watching as the eels stabbed at his boots. This was the final moment. The rope swung toward him.

He leapt, over the eels as they shuddered and writhed, blasting poison gas. Ja-Jaguar leapt as well, after Travis, it's nightmarish vectory thrusting it upward with surprising speed. He would likely be outpaced. All he saw was the rope. And there, he had it! He felt the coarse threading binding it together, how it wanted to splinter at his fingers as he gripped it for dear life. The mechanism span Travis just outside Ja-Jaguar's reach.

Travis released and flung himself safely to the dirty patch on the other side of the pit. He'd done it. Once more, he'd survived. And once more, Ja-Jaguar was not so lucky. Even propelled by whatever dark vectory had manifested within it, it could not survive the poisonous thrashing of the eels. They bit and stabbed at it, tearing at the remnants of its flesh.

Travis crept closer and peered over the side of the pit. There were only bubbles now- no sign of Ja-Jaguar. Not knowing how else to respond to the cat's demise, Travis made the Sign of the Fates. He raised his right hand forward and extended his thumb, index and middle fingers, while closing his ring finger and his pinkie. It was a sign of respect shared amongst people who followed the Fates.

The gesture was not returned by the murky pit. There was a splash, and a few small crocodiles appeared at the water's surface, staring at Travis and opening their mouths wide like he might be delicious. Travis turned away from the lizards and looked toward the new paths ahead of him. Once again Travis had three choices. Three different hallways sprang forth, to his right, to his left, and to the center. Deciding he might have a look down each before choosing one, Travis stepped forward on the central floor tile, or at least, what appeared to be tile. He realized immediately that the tile felt gritty, so he went down to inspect it for hidden writing. But when his fingers touched the surface of the dirt, they stuck. He struggled to remove them, and had to fight with all his force to do so. His legs however seemed permanently fixed to the substance, and were slowly sinking inside of it. Like a fool, Travis had stepped into a cleverly disguised quicksand patch. He looked for some way to free himself as he sank. That was when he heard a cawing from above, the flapping of wings. All at once the crows dove at him, four winged daggers plunging at his fingers as he sank further and further into the pit.

They bit and tore at his flesh, stabbing at him. He began to weep from the pain. He was slowly sinking. He could taste the mud in his own tears. The birds would not relent. They cawed, laughing at him, roaring triumphantly, and while they taunted him he grabbed two of them, one in each palm and slammed them downward into the mud with him.

The other birds screeched in horror. The one with the grey tuft on his leg began pecking at Travis's head, while the other flew down to try to free his comrades and ended up getting stuck in the mud as well. Travis grabbed at the overturned birds' legs, using them for leverage so he could pull himself just close enough to one of the sides of the pit that he could reach the small ridge that separated it from the labyrinth's stone tiles. As he reached the edge, his fingers bleeding and covered with feathers, the grey spotted crow leapt from atop his head and landed down by the edge of the pit so it could pick at his fingernails, disabling him from escaping.

That was when the unexpected happened. Travis could see the spotted crow jerk backward, as if it had been pulled by the tail.

As it lay prone in shock, its mouth agape, Travis saw the culprits. The small crocodiles that had looked at him so hungrily had crawled out of the pit and were now ripping at the spotted crow's tail feathers. As the crow realized what was happening, it scraped at the ground then turned and tried to peck at the crocodiles intimidatingly, but one of them happily clamped its jaws down on the big crow's neck and twisted like a wheel.

Travis realized his chest was nearly below the sand. He struggled and grunted, sinking a bit deeper, now one-handed, the other submerged in the muck, and with absolute precision, he dug his bloodied fingers into the edge of the tile nearest him. He pulled until he was free, the crocodiles finishing their meal and becoming interested in his fingers, then his shoes as he righted himself.

"Onward," he said, hoarse from shouting, kicking the crocodiles back into the pit whence they came.

Having a moment of thought to himself, he looked upward, checking to see if the crowd was still vehemently rooting for his death. But it seemed the crowd was oddly mixed in its reaction, creating a loud conversational murmur, mixtures of boos, some cheers, angry ranting, and many confused faces. Something had happened, unbeknownst to him, and it seemed as though public opinion wasn't quite so strictly opposed to his survival anymore. Travis sleepily smirked.

"What fair-weather friends you lot are," he said.

There were still three paths to choose from, and based on what he'd experienced so far, there was no telling which one was correct. The path to his left seemed wide and inviting, well-lit, but he had been through enough misleading passages already to know that looks could be deceiving. The narrow hall that led forward that made him feel slightly uneasy, like the walls might close in on him. The path to his right was dark and jutted off around a corner. It was definitely the scariest option.

"Travis," an odd female voice called to him from around that corner. It seemed to bounce along the walls to reach him.

"I'm not falling for your tricks," said Travis. "Whoever you are."

"Travis," it said in reply.

The voice sounded gentle but warbled like the voice of an elderly woman.

"You must listen to me," the voice spoke sternly to him. "Follow my voice."

This all sounded suspicious to Travis, but he was indeed curious. *How does this woman know my name? Kane told them I was Rat-Catcher.*

Travis turned along the path, following the echoing voice. The path met a painting hanging on the wall underneath a small awning. The painting was a still life of some immaculately sculpted, delicious looking fruit, sparkling in the gleaming sunlight. There was no sign of whoever had called him.

"Reveal yourself," Travis commanded.

There was no answer. Travis wanted to see if there was a trick to the painting, so he reached out to touch it. As his fingers crept closer toward it, jets of flame shot out from either side of the painting's frame, aiming toward Travis's fingers. Somehow the painting itself remained immaculate, even as the flames burned and seared its surface. Travis yelped and retreated. His fingers still felt hot.

Someone had called out to him, spoken to him. Had it been a trick of his own mind? *No*, he was certain that he'd heard it. Perhaps it came from another place in the maze? Or maybe there was another trick wall involved? But the voice had seemed to echo from down this hallway, as if a woman had been right there.

Travis wanted to believe she was somehow concealed within the painting, although that did not make any logical sense. *Could Ducat Duncan have incorporated vectory into the design of this maze?* Travis wondered. He had seemed so adamantly opposed to vectory. Still there was some otherworldly corruption at hand. How else could Ja-Jaguar have risen from the dead?

Travis stared at the painting. If he was quick enough he could touch it and rush his arm back to safety. He practiced a few times in the air. The fire might burn him, but surely he could survive a little burning? He suddenly remembered the heat from the fire in his childhood home and shuddered.

Travis shot his hand toward the painting's surface, and his fingers traveled right through it, into someplace different. A magical portal warbled with vectory around his wrist like the surface of a pond.

The flames burst forth around him. Soon his arm was engulfed, and he shrieked, trying to swat it out, until he realized most strangely of all that he was not in pain. He still felt the warm tingly sensation, like his arm had fallen asleep next to a cooling pie, but that was the end of the sensation. He stopped patting at it and let the flame burn his arm for a bit, before shaking it out.

"It's an illusion," he decided.

He reached back toward the painting slowly but felt no pain as the fire blazed. With a burst of courage, Travis dove through the painting into a world unknown.

THE WITCH

There was a room beyond the painting's artifice. It was an octagonal room of purple swirls. There were tufted silk rugs stacked high to his left and right. They towered over Travis ominously. It felt too tight to breathe. He leaned against them and they barely budged. In the center of the room, lit by a single candle was an elderly woman. She looked ancient but serene. Her mouth was covered with a veil. She wore white robes and a gold sash as if she were a priestess. She prayed before a small stone chalice filled with bright blue liquid. She did not move an inch even as Travis approached. Then, suddenly her bright blue eyes shot open.

"Travis Sebastian," she said. "Alive and well."

Travis did not feel well. *She said the name Sebastian,* Travis realized. *Who is this woman? How does she know me?*

She smiled through her veil so the curving corners of her mouth were visible. She twiddled a finger toward the chalice. Twin ribbons sprang forth from either side of her and clasped the cup, bringing it closer to her nose. She sniffed at the potion.

"I am a friend of Kane Verdalea," she said. "He thinks that he is very smart, but in truth, I am far smarter than he is. That is how I have found you."

Kane had warned him that there were forces working against them. Could this old woman be so knowledgeable because she was a spy of some sort?

"I see you do not trust me," she said. It sounded as though she was pouting a little. "That is no matter. I shall keep this accelerant to myself. Your vectory shall never be unleashed, and you will die in this maze, a skinny white skeleton."

Though her words were harsh, she sang them tauntingly.

"What's an accelerant?" asked Travis.

The old woman laughed. "Has Kane taught you so little? Yes, yes, he is a foul teacher. I will be your teacher instead." She shrieked with laughter.

Travis backed away from her, suddenly realizing that the portal into the painting was no longer visible behind him. There were just more rugs, no sign of an exit.

"Travis Sebastian," she repeated. "You would dare defy your teacher? I should punish you. But this is not my way. I have for you a present."

"What does it do?" asked Travis.

"You are a Vec, yes?" she asked. "But you are a baby Vec. Your power is weak like a baby plant within a seed. We must awaken the seed so the plant can grow."

The ribbons holding the chalice sailed toward him, gesturing the potion enticingly. It certainly smelled interesting, like blueberries mixed with mead, but how could he be certain it was not poison? He shook his head and smushed his lips shut.

Twin ribbons curled behind him and like a pair of pincers plucked a hair from his head. His eyes widened and his mouth shot open in pain. Then the chalice tipped forward into his mouth, flooding his senses with its overpowering vectory. He spasmed and shook as what felt like a cold rain coated him internally. His eyes felt like they were blinking, even though his eyelids weren't moving. Suddenly the pain that had been welling up from every ache in his muscles was relenting. The scrapes and cuts on his flesh were mending, and he felt reinvigorated, as though the potion were medicinal.

"You see?" the old woman asked. "It is good, yes? Like a sweet pie."

Travis did not know if he would compare the sensation to eating a pie, but he was at least convinced the woman had not poisoned him. He felt as though he had gotten a full night's rest in a moment's time.

"You will still need teaching in our ways," she explained. "But this will let the vectory within you flow freely."

She waved a withered old claw lazily and the portal reopened in the rugs behind him, turning the fabric stacks into a rippling liquid surface.

"I shall miss you dearly until next we meet, my sweet," the old woman said, as two ribbons grabbed Travis by the shoulders and tossed him through the portal.

Suddenly he was back at the end of the labyrinthian hallway, laying on the ground beneath the painting. The twin flames shooting from the painting's sides were still blazing, yet he was unharmed. The people in the balconies looked to be leaving, assuming Travis was dead and that the show was over. Once they saw him moving around, they roared with disbelief. The boy could not be stopped!

Travis rose to his feet, the effect of the potion still resonating within him. In his stomach he felt a cosmic pulse, as if he was being pointed in a particular direction. He knew immediately to head back toward the quicksand, but to take the middle path and definitely not the one that split to the left where there was something deadly lying in wait. Travis could feel the directional pulse beaming him toward the correct path. It felt cool and vibrant to follow the path.

Maybe it's a trick? What feels nice could be a lie, Travis thought.

He decided to test the feeling by heading in the direction that it had warned him about. As he traveled closer, a tingle vibrated through his entire body like an icy chill. In spite of this warning, Travis turned the corner to see a nice wooden chest with embezzlements on the side, a treasure waiting to be plundered.

Travis smiled. *I was right. The potion was another trick.*

Certain that he had made the right choice, Travis opened the chest, and a spider the size of a pig shot forward, pinning him on his back, trapping him to the stone tile with a web that it spat from its drooling mandibles. He clawed at the web and tried to get free, but it was too sticky to rip. The spider was lowering itself onto Travis very slowly. It moved its jaws above Travis's head, dripping green with saliva.

Travis screamed as he tried unsuccessfully to break the webbing.

"Away, you foul beast," a voice cried from above.

A small purple bat with Kane's voice rocketed toward the

spider, slamming it right in the eye. The spider squealed in pain and backed away, stumbling against a wall and collapsing.

"I'm so sorry, Travis," Kane the bat said, fluttering around Travis's face. "Oh, just look at you! Ducat's already sentenced you to death. I instilled my aura in this bat as soon as I heard the bells ringing. I don't know anything about echolocation and these tunnels are absolutely dreadful. How are you then? Holding up alright?"

The spider looked to be unconscious, but its legs were twitching as though that might be temporary. Travis struggled to free himself.

Kane fluttered about him, unhelpfully chattering away.

"To be honest," said Kane the bat, "I thought you might be a bit more restrained than to immediately get yourself sentenced to death the way you did. What did you do anyway? It must have been utterly shameful. You look hideous by the way."

"You left me to die," said Travis. "These people are animals!"

"What's wrong with animals, Travis?" Kane asked. "The human being is merely an animal that learned to speak and do commerce and so forth. Many animals are quite clever. Not this bat I've hypnotized though. He's an awful brute. Merely wants to eat rickticks all day. I'm sorry if that makes you hungry. I know the accommodations at the orphanage were not exactly transcendental."

Travis dragged himself out of the thick gooey webs that were cementing his legs to the floor and stood, staring angrily at the bat fluttering nearby.

"I say," Kane said. "Don't you dare eat me again!"

Before Travis could reply, a sticky web shot from the spider's mouth and trapped Kane's bat against the wall.

"Bah!" Kane shouted as the bat's eyes went spinning. "This disgusting creature!"

The greedy-looking spider chittered happily. It leapt to the web on the wall so it could loom over the bat villainously. It looked to be holding Kane's bat hostage. Travis took a deep breath and summoned his courage. He leapt forward, attempting to snatch the bat from the webbing, but the spider was too quick.

"Don't worry, Travis," the bat said. "It's just a b-"

And before Kane could finish, the spider gobbled him up. There was something about this spider that seemed familiar. Then the memory struck him.

"I remember you from my book of creatures," Travis shouted. "You're an arakid. You're mean, and greedy, and you gobble up everything in sight."

The arakid responded by belching out one of Kane's little purple wings in a pile of bright green spit-up. It fired a web directly at Travis, but he deftly dodged out of the way. *I need some sort of weapon,* he thought. *Something to pierce that spider's outer shell.* He scanned the area, but there was nothing usable in sight. The arakid was hissing and rearing backward like it aimed to charge at him. He retreated, nearly stumbling into the quicksand all over again.

He leapt over the sand trap, and the spider leapt too, just behind him. Travis headed for the only remaining hallway, the one that narrowed. He could hear the spider scuttling after him, hissing and spitting vile fluid.

The hallway ended in a maze within the maze, a series of flat wooden walls set into metal slits in the walls and floors. As Travis entered the new area of the labyrinth, replete with wooden divisions, three metal spears emerged from the floor behind him and sliced up into the air, creating a barrier that disabled him from escaping. The arakid tried to leap over the spears but incorrectly gauged their speed, impaling itself on the spears as they rose. The crowd gasped.

Travis could see that the maze had become vastly more complicated. The wooden planks created several paths for Travis to follow, and all were equally viable. The slits in the walls and floors troubled Travis enough that he did not move for fear of triggering something terrifying.

Badadat! Badadat! Badadat!

He could hear the sound of hooves and heavy breathing. It sounded as though a stallion were stampeding towards him. It was getting louder and louder, vibrating Travis's skull. Then it suddenly stopped. Before Travis could decide which way to run, the wooden walls around him slid into the ground. New ones slid upward from places where empty slits had been, creating a new configuration of the maze.

Where once there were walls there were now six stone statues. Each statue was designed to look like an intimidating knight with a demonic helmet. They were archers, each pointing tar-soaked arrows. As they dripped, Travis realized that without moving, the trap had already sprung around him. The tips of the arrows immolated and fired forward. Travis threw his body under them as they crossed paths overhead. He narrowly escaped singeing his hindquarters. He hit the ground hard, slowing his breathing. Travis decided not to stick around and see if the archers would reload. He continued onward in the maze, carefully watching the walls and floors for transformations.

Once again the pounding sounded, like thunderous cloven hooves trampling a mountainside, echoing against the walls of the labyrinth. Travis closed his eyes and focused on the power within him, now terrified that whatever was making that sound might appear. He felt the weird pulsing in his stomach, then a strange quiver, a warble. He could feel the potion's effects still burrowing within him somehow. It did not hurt, but it felt like a foreign presence with a consciousness of its own. He had been so desperate to disprove the vectory before, but now, bereft of clear advantage and fearing for his life, he decided it might be time to commune with it. The power throbbed like a heart-beat, but when he focused, he saw that it only pointed him toward the exit, as if the changing slats had somehow confused it. It wished him to go through the wood itself, which would of course be impossible. *GR-GR-GR-GR-GR.* The walls began moving again. As they slid away, an axe came slicing through the air near Travis's head.

He ducked, but it felt like some of his hair had not survived the maneuver. The blade of the axe pinned the shorn locks to the wall before releasing them and swinging high over its wielder's head. This creature was not human, though it had oddly human eyes, heartfelt and brown, darting slightly with debate. Its face was that of a deer though shaggy and striped darkly. Its antlers split in four directions from its skull like an elk's, with tips that reached out in clawed hands at the sky. From above he looked like a deadly four-leaf clover. And so the people of Southerner's Roost had named him Clover, the Four-Leaf Cleaver.

THE FOUR-LEAF CLEAVER

Clover was the champion of the labyrinth. He represented its brutality. No one had survived the labyrinth since Clover had been made its final challenge. No knight had been knighted since Clover was discovered outside the city limits three months prior, drunk and disoriented, wildly swinging his axe. They threw him in the labyrinth for sport, but Clover solved it so quickly that they had to come up with another plan. They could not have this creature clearly comprised of vectory serve as a knight. And so they forced him to live in the labyrinth as its champion, rewarding him for defeating all who challenged him in combat.

Clover's axe blade glinted in the torchlight as he brought it down toward Travis's skull once more, roaring bestially. Travis dove and scrambled through Clover's legs, darting behind him. Clover's axe blade nearly caught Travis as he scampered away. The blade embedded itself into a wooden slat, and Clover struggled to free it while shouting at Travis over his shoulder.

"Come back here," Clover roared. "I'm not playing hide-and-seek!"

The fact that the creature could talk only terrified Travis further. This wasn't some thoughtless beast, but a cold, calculating murderer. He narrowly avoided smashing into a wall as he charged down a corridor, hoping to make some progress before the maze changed again.

"Clover, Clover," the crowd chanted. “Chop his head. Grind him dead.”

Travis stopped short of bashing his nose into a rising wall. Clover was grunting and snorting, shaking a bit of drool from his jowls. Travis ran around a corner toward the opposite side of the maze, Clover chasing him like a bad nightmare.

About midway down the hall, the walls changed again, and Travis caught sight of a gilded treasure chest with red leather on its lid. He ran toward it, crouching to open it, hoping for a weapon. As Clover approached him from behind, the walls closed around Travis, encasing him in a wooden cube.

A lucky break, Travis thought. He only had a few seconds to open the box before the walls shifted again and led him straight back into the fray. He opened the lid and a fleet of frogs leapt out and began pummeling him with their surprisingly vicious legs. He groaned and flailed, pulling them off of his person and tossing them back in the chest one at a time. It became quite the hassle, as they kept leaping back out.

The crowd roared as the walls shifted and their hero Clover swung his axe wildly. Travis ducked, but one of the frogs was liquified by the sailing blade.

Clover's axe kept sailing and smashed into another wooden wall which had remained in position during the latest switch. Now the axe was stuck again, halfway through the wall. Travis recognized his cue for departure and bolted.

"You keep running and you’ll really tick me off,” Clover

screamed.

As he ran Travis tried to concentrate on the feeling of vectory within him. *Yes,* he thought, visualizing the path out of the labyrinth. He was close now. He had inadvertently headed in the correct direction after barreling around at random. *But surely the walls will shift again to prevent me from escaping,* he thought. *I need a way of distracting the beast first.* And just as Travis was forced to make a decision between heading toward the exit or away from it, Clover leapt out from behind a shifting wall and tossed his entire axe so that it spun handle over blade in the air. Time slowed to quarter-speed as Travis dodged to the side, narrowly evading the spinning axe. He could feel the vectory powering him now, allowing him to move more deftly than he'd ever been able to move before.

"You are an oily little rat," Clover bellowed.

"Then why are you having so much trouble?" Travis asked.

"You will die by my hands," Clover shouted, leaping toward Travis, meaning to choke him to death.

Travis screamed and ran around another corner, heading backward, away from the exit but away from Clover as well.

Clover was charging toward Travis, lowering his head so that his quartet of antlers were pointed toward the boy, ready to flay the skin off his body upon impact. After a few twists and shifts, a wall appeared directly between Travis and Clover, effectively segmenting their chase. Travis kept going, but breathed a sigh of relief.

"Oh blessed Fates," he said.

KRACK!

The wall had been too weak for Clover's billowing might! He'd bashed through it and was grunting and charging toward Travis, his eyes barely focusing, blurring with hatred. Travis moaned as he continued running, Clover at his heels.

Clover grabbed at Travis, and his hairy clawed fingers tore at Travis's garments. Travis rounded a corner, and Clover cut the corner by plowing through it. The walls shifted again. Travis felt now that he had a basic understanding of their timing, but fear pounded in his brain like a headache.

There was a dead end ahead, but if Travis guessed correctly, he might be able to plan something. Feeling a shift about to occur, Travis ran to the end of the wall, and pantomimed trying to climb it desperately, waiting for Clover to follow. Clover slowed his pace and breathed deeply. He was taking his time now.

"Yes," he said. "Submit to your execution."

Clover lurched forward as the walls began to change. Travis dove for the opening in the walls as one opened and another began to close, narrowly scraping his stomach over a wall that was rising up. Clover slammed against the wall as it closed behind Travis, too enervated to bash his way through.

Travis headed onward, toward a stone wall shaped like a skull. Travis ran forward and pressed a stone where the skull's nose was. The stone slid in, and a wall near Travis gave way. From behind the wall a barking dog, grey and porcine came racing forth. Just before it reached Travis it stopped, held in place by a chain leash.

Travis, undeterred by the dog's ferocity, spied the path of the dog's leash, which appeared to be tied to some sort of mechanism. As the dog strained on its leash, the mechanism slowly turned, and the dog could reach closer to Travis. The wooden maze shifted again. Travis heard the thudding of Clover's hooves.

"Do not hide from me, you irritating child," called Clover. "If I do not kill you, they will not feed me, and every second I go hungry means another drop of blood I will spill. Do you hear me, you coward?!"

Travis couldn't see Clover over the wooden walls, but based on the proximity of Clover's voice, Travis knew that he needed to move fast. The grey hound barked savagely and pulled the mechanism again, leading itself closer to Travis. That was when Travis spied the iron sword on the floor between the dog's hind legs and the slit in the wall where its chain led.

If I could just get that sword, he thought. He could feel the flame of vectory pulsating within him. *Yes*, Travis thought. As he concentrated on that feeling, the one that had felt like static electricity that could rise and swell in his brain if he forced it to, he could see the droplets of spit flying off the piggish dog's lips. Its barks became elongated sounds that drowned into the background noise, the chanting of the people watching him. All were unified in the endless noise of existence, everything in entropy, screaming in unison. He could hear it.

Travis could hear Clover clomping, the chain leash clinking as the dog pulled at it. Whatever was embedded in the wall was slowly letting it free as it pulled harder and harder, though the strain seemed to be exerting great counterforce against the dog. Then the walls shifted again. Travis heard Clover's heavy breathing. He could feel the beast just beyond the walls. Should he move too loudly, the beast might come crashing through to grab him.

Should Clover get the sword, Travis thought, *I'm truly dead.*

Travis darted down a newfound path in the wooden slats and turned a corner. As he continued running, the dog chomped at the air and barked after him, wrestling with the machine that bound it.

Travis saw that he had made a bit of a circle, as evidenced by the slash marks and broken walls. He followed the path a bit further to find Clover's battle-axe laying on the ground.

Travis ran toward it and tried to lift it, but it was too heavy for him pull the blade off the ground. He could hear Clover stomping to his right, and as the walls shifted again Travis dragged the axe in the opposite direction. He rounded another corner and came face-to-face with Clover.

"That's my axe," Clover said, "you little thief. You are too scrawny to even wield it! Give it here, so I may end your life and claim the pittance I am offered."

The walls switched again, enclosing Clover and Travis in a rectangular cell. Travis dragged the blade backward, further and further away from Clover, now feeling truly trapped. Travis could imagine an antler skewering him, one of Clover's fangs stabbing at his neck. All he had left within him was a prayer to whatever vectory the witch had unleashed.

He closed his eyes and he could see the hovering face of death. *The skull,* he realized. Praying to the Fates, he concentrated on the yellow aura of electricity within him. He could feel it charging, slowly growing and gaining power, forming a tactile grabbing claw, and with this imaginary electric arm, he reached out, and took the axe within his grasp. Suddenly his own muscles were empowered with the divinity of the pulsating aura, charging his body, enabling it to lift more than it ever had before. Clover was inches away from Travis, but with a sudden surge of might, Travis swung the battle axe and lopped an antler clean off of Clover's head.

Clover tumbled toward the wall, shocked by the loss of his antler and the sudden strength of the boy. Travis was also surprised by his strength. He felt the weight of the axe once more and dropped it, backing away from Clover.

“You’ve ruined my head,” Clover shouted. “I’m hideous!”

Clover ran toward his axe, plucked it off the ground and cornered Travis. The walls began to rumble. Travis dodged toward his right, but it was a poor choice. This wall remained in place, while the one on the other side slid into the floor.

"Your luck ran out," Clover said. “Finally, I will taste victory!”

And as he brought down the blade, the grey hound lunged at Clover's throat, biting and clawing at his chest, knocking him off balance. It had appeared from the passage that had just opened, still straining at its leash but well within range to give Clover a thrashing. Clover’s axe was knocked off balance as the dog tore at his arm. Clover tangled with the canine, trying to free himself. In the chaos, Travis followed the dog’s leash and snagged the iron sword off the ground.

Ark, the dog whined as Clover kicked it away.

“Stupid dog,” said Clover. “You steal my table scraps!”

Clover prepared to strike Travis. Travis closed his eyes and concentrated on the electrical current within him. His arm tilted the iron blade and swung it to meet Clover's axe, deflecting a two-handed strike deftly.

Clover snorted with amazement.

"Are you a Vec?" he asked. "This isn't fair to me. You are cheat-ing."

"I'm cheating?!" Travis exclaimed. "You're a monster."

"My appearance is not fair game for your mockery!" Clover yelled. "I was once more handsome than you can ever imagine!"

Clover swung his axe again, and once more Travis deflected the blade. Travis fought and parried Clover, feeling the power of his aura guiding his movements. A yellow lightning bolt was slinking its way down the blade of his sword. Clover became uneasy about his proximity to such vectory, and relented in his offense, taking a step backward. Travis took this opportunity to chop off another antler.

Clover roared with displeasure, charging at Travis and swinging his axe. Travis bashed Clover's axe backward. The electricity at the end of Travis's blade burst forth and erupted, knocking Clover backward as well. Clover fell to the ground, groggy, but still clawing desperately at his axe.

"You want to lose that arm?" Travis asked.

Clover growled and relented, laying his remaining antlers against the dirt.

Travis knew from the crowd roaring overhead that this was the moment they'd waited for, the moment when the hero would slay the beast. He could feel the hatred and the lust for violence in their voices.

"Do it," said Clover. "End my wretched life. This life of blood and slavery."

Travis inhaled a breath. He raised his sword and threw it atop Clover's axe. Empty handed, he reached out to Clover to help him off the floor.

"I refuse," Travis said, "to become as cruel-hearted and hateful as these people want me to be. I refuse to treat you the way that they have treated me. All of us are rats, worms to these people. They want us to suffer so they can have a laugh. Well, I'm not going to give them what they want!"

Travis gestured to the people cheering wildly in the balcony. "Do you want to be their monster? Or do you want to prove them wrong?! Let's get out of here. Together. Make our own destinies."

Travis stared at Clover, begging him to consider the offer. Clover regarded Travis's outstretched arm like an infected tentacle. He snorted, then placed his head back down and laughed hysterically.

"I wish you had killed me before you spoke," he said.

"You don't have to be what they want you to be," said Travis.

Clover pulled himself upright.

"I do not need redemption in your eyes, or their eyes," he said. "To kill a warrior in battle is noble. If they realize you are a Vec, there will be no nobility. They will tear you apart limb from limb. When they tire of me they will eat me."

"That's ridiculous," said Travis.

"Go!" Clover ordered him. "You have won in combat. That means

I go hungry. Leave me before I take my vengeance."

"Fates save you," Travis said. He gave Clover the sign of the Fates.

Clover laid his head back down on the ground.

"Piss on the Fates," said Clover. "Pray to your ale."

SPELLBOUND SWORD

The whole thing seemed painfully unfair to Travis. Was there no place in this world free from suffering? Travis had desired to leave his own suffering behind, to be free from Vonkenschtook, but the world beyond Mercy Square was just as cruel. Maybe being trapped in the labyrinth had forced Clover to lose all faith. It seemed a sad state of affairs for any creature. This whole maze is an exercise in cruelty, Travis thought. And cruelty was what Ducat Duncan admired.

As he shuffled his feet toward the maze's exit, two spear-topped metal gates swung open, leading Travis toward a well-lit rounded tunnel that would likely take him back to the surface. When Travis crossed the final threshold, the crowd erupted in wild applause. This scrawny lad had beaten Clover!

"Rat-Catcher," they chanted.

And how funny it was, Travis thought, that crossing from one end to the other of a labyrinth had swayed their favor. Though Travis had struggled and nearly died to accomplish the feat, it seemed little more than chance, perhaps the will of the Fates, that had saved him. He could not be arrogant now, not after realizing that his success would mean Clover's starvation, that more people would be forced to compete in this hellish maze down the line. Travis's body ached, and he gritted his teeth, emulating Clover's own overbite in his disillusionment.

A cavalcade of knights charged toward Travis, swarming him, screaming and hooting and slapping him wildly. He had apparently impressed them as well.

"Rat-Catcher," they screamed.

Travis wondered if he should feel proud to befriend the men who had earlier that evening rejected him and sentenced him to death. They slapped him and raised him on their shoulders and cheered "Rat-Catcher" until their lungs were hoarse. Bewildered but feeling relatively safe now and physically exhausted, Travis allowed them to parade him around to the crowd's delight. After a few minutes, Ducat Duncan came riding down the slope of the tunnel on his horse.

He climbed off his steed, and the men placed Travis on the ground so he could speak to their lord with equal footing. Ducat still towered over Travis, but Travis no longer felt intimidated. *Perhaps that was the power of the labyrinth*, Travis thought, *to provide a knight the courage to conquer his fears*. And yet one woe remained in the back of Travis's mind. He sighed deeply.

"My boy," said Ducat, slapping a gauntlet on Travis's shoulder with force. "You have bested a maze that has taken the lives of men twice your age. You have evaded its traps, even defeated its champion. In truth, you are the first to beat Clover since he was chosen as the successor to our last, who was slain by Kingston four months ago in his own besting of the labyrinth."

Travis was surprised to hear this. He turned to Kingston who nodded firmly.

"That man, that Kane Verdalea," Ducat said, pacing and gesturing with a smile. "I feel so foolish to have mistrusted him. Here I thought he was trying to pawn off some damnable wretch, but look at you now! You have survived, and shall become a knight in my army. What do you say? Yes, you are humbled with gratitude."

Ducat paused from his pacing to lock eyes with Travis. Travis swallowed and nodded, unsure of how to proceed.

"My boy," said Ducat, taken aback by Travis's demeanor, "Are you not pleased with your own success? Perhaps the name Rat-Catcher strikes your ear like a dagger? To be frank, I care little for it, and find it ill-suiting. Perhaps the Jack Rabbit would be a better pseudonym. Your quickness and agility are surely your strong suit. Then again, you wielded a sword like a natural against our Clover. Shall I let you decide upon your own nickname? Knights are awarded special privileges. For example, I shall take into consideration your suggestion on where to be placed amongst my guard. In addition, it is customary for a knight to be awarded a small trinket from amongst my treasures. You've likely already spied something that interests you. By the Fates, I wonder if Verdalea's theory was right all along? This could be the future of military strategy!"

"My lord," said Kingston. "Forgive me for my impertinence, but some in the crowd have suggested there may have been vectory at play."

A small contingent of similarly stern knights nodded.

"Vectory?" Ducat asked, seeming genuinely puzzled. "Oh, the bit with the colorful theatrics? Well did you not see the poison that had infected Ja-Jaguar? He had been teeming with it when we brought him in from those damnable ruins. I'd hoped distance from that nightmarish place might cure the infection. But no, he infected my maze with his vectory as well. No matter. Now that he is dead, the matter should be resolved. The boy's blade must have been infected as well, so we shall have it destroyed. That should satisfy you all."

The knights considered this explanation, but Kingston did not seem convinced. Travis barely knew how to respond. Kingston was still staring at him stonily.

"I wish for you to free Clover," said Travis. "It's not right to trap people, to treat them like filth. I've suffered my whole life. I don't wish it on anybody."

Ducat was stunned. The rest of the knights stared slack-jawed, like the kid had just kicked his savior in the teeth.

"Such a strange request," Ducat muttered. "To release an abomination. If that is your wish, then I shall take it as your favor. He shall be released in the swamps. The people of Southerner's Roost have witnessed your birth as a hero. I should think you will serve as a fine mascot yourself."

"Thank you, um, great Ducat," said Travis.

"What of your trinket?" Ducat asked. "Most of my knights must visit my treasure hall later, but you've had the pleasure of seeing it today."

"The sword," Travis said. "I must have that sword."

Ducat sputtered with exasperation.

"My boy," Ducat said. "You are in danger of testing my patience. Perhaps one does not know the meaning of the word trinket? You are demanding the prized jewel of my museum. I should not part with it under any circumstances. Should I die, it shall be buried with me, as a reminder of my great nobility. I know because of the price I paid at auction that it is the most valuable treasure I own. Think instead of my lesser jewels, gems and broaches you may have spied. A lowly child like you would no doubt be happy with a satchel of shiny nails."

A pang of distress warbled in Travis's gut. There was no chance Ducat would part with the sword. *Perhaps I will have to steal it after all. But how?* He was too exhausted to consider a heist. He sighed deeply.

"I apologize, milord," said Travis, "if my request offended you. I knew not of your customs. Rather than a trinket of any kind, I request a position as a guard of your Treasure Hall so I may gaze upon that sword every day. Thinking of its beauty is what guided me toward the exit, when I had nothing left to give."

Ducat smiled, appreciating Travis's words.

"But great Ducat," Kingston interjected, "such positions are awarded to senior knights only. Has this child impressed you so thoroughly?"

Ducat considered this, then pointed to the crowd above. They were still celebrating Travis's victory, now rallying behind the tiny hero as the city's latest sensation.

"The people of Southerner's Roost have spoken," Ducat replied. "Once the people of Clockwork City hear this tale, we're sure to have a visit from royalty. You know how the Queen feels about celebrities. She is always hungry for the latest news. In lieu of a broach or pendant, the Rat-Catcher shall be given the prized seat of treasury guardsman. Come. We need to bathe you and prepare your armor. I suspect my subjects will be champing at the bit to meet you."

Ducat led Travis to the knight quarters, where he was given a tub of water in which to bathe. Afterward he rested on a cot neatly prepared for his use alone. Over the course of a few hours,

Ducat's blacksmith scrounged up a set of armor for Travis. The pieces were overlarge, but the effect was clear. Travis spied himself in a mirror and was shocked to see himself so fortified.

"I look like a knight got shrunk," said Travis.

The other knights laughed.

"You'll grow into them," Kingston grumbled.

When he was dressed for the occasion, they led him upstairs. In Ducat's main hall they had prepared a ceremony with the cleanest, most pristine people of Southerner's Roost attending. Ducat recited a long speech about the importance of knightly honor and the necessity of hardship and cruelty. The eyes of the crowd watched Travis closely, enamored with the boy who had survived their cruelty.

Travis tried to ignore their stares and focus on Ducat's speech, but the words all felt hollow to him. He was barely conscious during the rest of the evening. All he remembered was a delicious feast that put him into a sleepy stupor.

In the days that followed, Travis was given basic training by the guards. It consisted of combat drills with wooden dummies, rigorous etiquette lessons about knightly decorum, and an extensive series of lectures about the proper behavior of a treasury guardsman. Even though the job seemed to entail nothing but standing near priceless relics for many hours at a time, Travis could not escape these lectures about his duties, all of which came from a frail and aging knight named Poineswill who had served as a treasury guardsman for years.

No one told me being a knight would be so tedious, thought Travis.

There were no wars going on, and being that Southerner's Roost was rather remote, it seemed like the purpose of Ducat's army was to seem important. Though he never wished to return to the labyrinth, Travis began to miss the challenges found in life's chaotic mysteries. The only mystery to Travis's new duty was whether or not anyone would notice if he fell asleep with his helmet's visor down.

It did feel good to be closer to the sword that his parents had left him. The strange secret feeling of vectory amplified whenever he stepped near it. In the days Travis spent next to the sword, he would study its inscriptions, all of which were carved in strange geometric spirals along its hilt and blade. He had never seen anything like them before, but to be so close to the sword yet unable to touch it was torture. Whenever he crept too close to the case, the elderly knight Poineswill would lecture him severely about duty and cleanliness.

And so it came to be that Travis accepted his fate as a treasury guardsman. He had heard nothing of Kane since being knighted. In preparation for their next interaction, Travis decided that he should explore the feeling of vectory within himself, as it was no doubt the key to unleashing the sword's power.

He consistently felt a warm pulse emanating from the sword, as if a familial hearth was beckoning him to stay beside it. When Travis closed his eyes, he could shutter away the distractions of the jewels around him, even ignore the sword's golden sheen, and focus instead on the energy within it. When he concentrated on that vectory, he could feel a vibration of excitement from it, like it could tell he was honing in on its power. It felt like connecting with a long-lost friend.

One day when Travis was concentrating on that tingling electricity in his mind, he heard a choking gurgle and a squeaky flail, as if Poineswill was struggling.

Travis's eyes shot open, and there was Poineswill dancing about with anxiety, his gaze focused clearly on the golden sword which had illuminated with vectory. Strange multi-colored pulsating lines had filled its runic indentations. The sword gave off a light of its own. Poineswill could barely speak.

"Stop," cried Poineswill helplessly. "Vectory is forbidden!"

Poineswill approached Travis to reprimand him, but turned pale and stopped walking. Poineswill's eyes rolled back in his noggin and he emitted a strange groan. He collapsed suddenly in a clatter on the floor.

Travis gasped, and the light from the sword faded. Travis rushed over to see if he could rouse Poineswill, but nothing he could do would wake the man. There seemed to be breath coming from Poineswill's mouth and nose, so Travis knew the man yet lived, but there was no certainty that the old knight was well. Forgetting the sword for his human decency, Travis swung open the treasury doors and spoke to the two knights guarding the exterior. They quickly grabbed Poineswill and carried him toward the infirmary. Though the situation felt odd to Travis, the other knights saw no particular peculiarity in it.

"Fear not, Rat-Catcher," said one of the knights. "Poineswill has served many years. We all must depart for the Fates' domain at some point. And perhaps it was simply a fainting spell. My granny suffers them."

Travis still felt vaguely responsible for Poineswill's fall, but of course he could not mention this fact without revealing the sword's vectory. As the other knights carried Poineswill off, Travis realized his exact situation. He was the lone guard left on duty. *He was alone with the sword.*

He quickly re-entered the treasury and closed the door behind him. He approached the sword and concentrated on it with all of his might. Sure enough, the pulsing energy reached out to him again. Images of verdant fields, a cottage on a hilltop, lilies and marigolds, and the sounds of spring chirped in his mind's eye.

And then with a devastating shatter that would echo in his mind forever, the sword surged with energy and broke free from its bindings, swinging swiftly in the air of its own volition. The glass case shattered and sent fractals of bending light in every direction, causing shadows and runic symbols to dance across the treasure hall.

Travis ducked to avoid the sword's strike. And there it hung in the air, slowly rotating like a dancer's pirouette. Travis realized that the power surging from the sword wanted to speak to the power within him. The sword was a prisoner too. It had a magical life within it, and it longed to be with Travis.

Trusting the sensation emanating from the sword, Travis reached out and grabbed its hilt. He caught wind of a floral fragrance and felt the sensation that his arm had somehow become complete. His gauntlets slid into position like they were completing a long forgotten puzzle.

And then with a power Travis could no longer control, the sword warbled with vectory and lifted him toward the ceiling. He cried out in surprise, his legs dangling in the air as the sword slowly circled around the room like a vulture. Travis's boots banged against some of the other trophy cases as the sword pulled him around in a circle, gaining speed and momentum. Travis tried hard to be brave in spite of this singularly unknown sensation. Just as the sword reached a speed so fast that Travis felt his hold might break, the sword charged forth, bursting through a nearby window and carrying Travis high into the sky outside of Southerner's Roost, past the clouds and soaring geese. He was airborne, free, propelled by the vectory of the sword. And there was no turning back.

Made in the USA
Monee, IL
18 January 2020